FOUND BY THE ALPHA

ID JOHNSON

For Lisa

CONTENTS

Chapter 1 The Pain   vii

Chapter 2 Help   xi

Chapter 3 Footprints   xv

Chapter 4 Checking In   xix

Chapter 5 Foreign   xxiii

Chapter 6 Mercy   xxvii

Chapter 7 Introductions   xxxi

Chapter 8 Awake   xxxv

Chapter 9 Social   xxxix

Chapter 10 Finders Keepers   xliii

Chapter 11 Shards   xlvii

Chapter 12 Calm   li

Chapter 13: Plan   1

Chapter 14 Lists   5

Chapter 15 Pizza   9

Chapter 16: Safe and Happy   13

Chapter 17 Sleepless Night   17

Chapter 18 Like China   21

Chapter 19 Overwhelm   25

Chapter 20 Roomie   29

Chapter 21: Covers   33

Chapter 22: Unboxed   37

Chapter 23: Lid   41

Chapter 24 Drip   45

Chapter 25 Breakfast   49

Chapter 26: No Poker Face   53

Chapter 27 The Village   57

Chapter 28: Danger Zone   61

Chapter 29 The Explorer   65

Chapter 30: Rush   69

Chapter 31: The Darkness   73

Chapter 32: Not a Dream   77

Chapter 33: Brush   81

Chapter 34: Problems   85

Chapter 35: Not Possible   89

Chapter 36: Coffee Confidential   93

Chapter 37: Out   97

Chapter 38 Trapped Inside   101

Chapter 39: She-Wolf   105

Chapter 40: Out of the Box   109

Chapter 41: Sobs   113

Chapter 42: Take Me   117

Chapter 43: The Next Morning   121

Chapter 44: Awkward   125

Chapter 45: The Story   129

Chapter 46: Telling Mercy   133

Chapter 47: More Guests   137

Chapter 48: Premonition   141

Chapter 49: Coffee with a Stranger   145

Chapter 50: Battle Prep   149

Chapter 51: Not the Luna Yet   153

Chapter 52: Heavy Thoughts   157

Chapter 53: A New Job   161

Chapter 54: Sealed With a Kiss and More   165

Chapter 55: Being the Luna   169

Chapter 56: Knocks in the Night   173

Chapter 57: Night Battle   177

Chapter 58: No Mercy   181

Chapter 59: Face Off   185

Chapter 60: Track Down   189

Chapter 61: Battle's End   193

Epilogue   197

Also by ID Johnson   201

CHAPTER 1 THE PAIN

Pain. All she could feel was pain--immeasurable, all-consuming pain that radiated all through her body, from the tips of her fingers and toes to the top of her head. As much as she wanted to go on, to continue, there was nothing more she could do. Having already fallen to the ground, in utter exhaustion, she found her will was not enough to lift her agonizing body up off of the leaf covered forest floor. Her eyes wouldn't even open, so how in the world could she possibly manage to get her disagreeable limbs to push up from her prone position and continue on her way. No, she wasn't going anywhere.

As she lay there, darkness overcoming her, the wind stirring what was left of her cropped, dark hair, the idea that she couldn't quite recall what she was running from came to mind. All she could remember was that she was afraid, deathly afraid, and having seen an opportunity to run, she'd done exactly that. Now, having fallen more times than she could count, striking her head on a tree trunk and then on the cold, hard ground, the memories of what she was fleeing had somehow shaken loose so that she couldn't remember much of anything at all. Fuzzy thoughts filled her mind, as she faded away, not even her own name coming to mind.

The crunching of leaves in the distance brought her around, along with a strong odor, one that was vaguely familiar, but not quite the same as the one that was secreted away in the back of her mind. That overwhelming sense that she needed to run filled her mind again, but her body refused to cooperate. She was not going anywhere. If those approaching were truly the ones that she was running from, she was doomed to be taken back to wherever it was she'd worked so hard to escape from.

"What is that?" A whispery voice filled her mind, and she realized she wasn't hearing this voice with her ears. Rather, it was coming to her through her mind, something she'd only heard about before but was fairly sure she'd never experienced, not that her memories had come back to her. They hadn't. Still, this seemed unfamiliar.

"It's a girl," another voice said. "Or… a woman."

"Where the hell did she come from?" a third voice asked, this one male and louder than the other two.

"Who the hell knows," the first voice said. This one was a male also, but not as strong as the other--more hesitant. "She looks like she's in pretty bad shape."

"We need a healer." That was the second voice again, a female.

"A healer? For all we know, she's a human." The loud male seemed very close to her now. She tried to open her eyes, to look at him, but no matter how hard she tried to move her eyelids, nothing happened.

"We can't just leave her here. Besides, she doesn't smell like a human, not exactly," the gentler of the males said.

Their voices started to blend together as her mind went fuzzy again, and the next thing she knew, she felt something warm and soft against her body, and then even though she truly would've rather lied there in the woods and died, she was being lifted and could tell they were moving her though she was unable to open her eyes or say anything at all to let them know how much everything hurt and how grateful she would be if death just claimed her now.

As her mind began to fade again, it occurred to her that though she had initially feared these creatures, because of their similarities to whomever she'd been running from, these were not the ones who'd harmed her and caused her to run away. No, as she was carried away, potentially toward healing and safety, her last, jumbled thoughts were that perhaps these creatures were not so bad after all.

CHAPTER 2 HELP

"Quickly, carry her in here!"

August Reeves heard a commotion outside of his office as he sat behind his desk, looking over a treaty a neighboring pack had sent to him a few days ago. They wanted hunting rights on a hundred acres of his northern territory, in exchange for no longer disputing a border they'd been contentious about for centuries, something he was considering granting them, but when he heard the chaos going on outside of his office, he was lured outside, leaving the papers behind.

A band of his Omegas were walking by, quickly, carrying what appeared to be the body of a small, unconscious woman with them. His mother, the pack healer and acting Luna, Isabella, was motioning for them to hurry and get the woman to the clinic. Though his pack, Rising Moon, held over six hundred members, August was almost positive he'd never seen this woman before, even though he couldn't see her face from the angle she was being carried.

He hurried along behind them, almost forgetting to close the door to the small office building behind him as he went. That wouldn't do. There were papers in there not just anyone needed to see. As he rushed after the trio, he called for his Beta, Beaux Thibodeau, to meet him at the clinic, using the mind-link. Whatever was going on, Beaux would need to know about it, too.

He caught up to them just as his mother was pulling back the curtain to one of the roped off areas, directing the others to lay the woman down on a hospital bed. There were no other patients in the clinic at the time, which was a good thing. It looked like this woman was going to need all of the attention his mother had to give.

"What's going on?" August asked, pausing near the door. The three Omegas who'd been out patrolling on the eastern border were some of his best. Ronnie, Sidney, and Grant were fast and not afraid of anything. They stood back away from the bed now, their eyes flickering from the young lady to their leader and back again as they fought to control their breath and speak.

"We found her lying out in the woods about three hundred meters from the border with Black Hole Moon Pack," Ronnie explained. He was sweating from exertion, not that the girl was big, but it was clear the three of them had been in a rush to get her back here.

"What happened to her?" August asked. He looked at the woman for a moment and noticed, even though she was covered with dry blood and bruises, and her dark hair looked as if it had recently been chopped off by someone who had no business wielding a pair of scissors, she was quite pretty. He tried not to stare at her as his mother was checking her vitals and returned his attention to the three rescuers.

Sidney shook her head, her long, curly brown hair dancing over her muscular shoulders as she did so. "We're not sure. She was just lying there, unconscious, covered in blood and bruises. She smelled like she might belong to a nearby pack, but we thought, if she was running through the woods in her human form, she must be afraid of something."

"How do you know she was running in her human form?" August asked, taking a few steps closer as he ran his hand through his caramel blond hair. This entire situation smelled like trouble to him.

"Her feet," Grant explained. "They're torn all to hell. She'd obviously been running for a while with no shoes on. Clearly, human feet are not meant to take that sort of a beating."

He wondered if she was even a shifter. Why would anyone run through the forest with no shoes on when they could utilize a wolf's paws, which were meant to carry them over the rugged terrain of the woods?

"She's definitely a shifter," his mother said from her perch on the edge of the bed next to the girl. "But… there's also quite a bit wrong with the poor dear. She has bruises, both old and new, as well as cuts and scrapes in all stages of healing. I can tell she's had some broken bones in the past as well, though I don't think any of them are currently broken. Her shoulder seems to be out of its socket. That will need resetting, which is horribly painful. Still, I think she is one of us. Just not sure where she's from. She doesn't quite seem like she belongs to Black Hole, does she?"

"What's going on?" Beaux arrived, stepping in behind August, just in time to miss everything Isabella had just explained. "Who's that?"

"That's what we'd like to know," August said, patting his second on the shoulder.

"Maybe we should contact Black Hole and see if they're missing anyone?" Grant suggested.

"Are you crazy?" Sidney spoke up. "For all we know, all of those scars and bruises are from some asshole over at Black Hole. The last thing we want to do is hand her back over. No way. We wait until she wakes up and then ask her who she is and what happened."

Both Omegas looked at August, waiting for him to tell them which of them was right. He caught his mother's eyes, and she nodded slowly. "Yes, let's wait," he said, agreeing with Sidney. "Let's see what she can tell us first. When she wakes up."

His mother's face fell, and a grim expression overtook her as she said, "If she wakes up."

CHAPTER 3 FOOTPRINTS

August stepped outside with his three Omegas and his Beta, Beaux, so that they could tell him more about what had happened. He did his best to listen, but his mind kept going back to the woman inside of the Health Center. She looked so frail, so weak. His mother was a talented healer, and if anyone could find a way to help the girl, it was Isabella, but she was so broken, as his mother had said, she just might never wake up.

"She was just lying there, you know?" Grant was saying. "So still. I thought she was dead."

"She wasn't moving at all," Sidney reiterated. "It was frightening."

"We had to shift to get her back here," Ronnie continued. "We found some clothes in a narrowed out hollow tree and shifted so we could carry her back. If she'd been even a little bit conscious, we might've been able to get her on one of our backs, but we were afraid she'd fall off."

August nodded. All of that made sense. "Why don't you guys show me where you found her?" he suggested.

"Sure. We need to get back on patrol anyway. We let the guards know we were coming in so they could keep an eye out, but it's our turn to run the perimeter," Sidney explained. August was impressed that they'd seemed to think of everything, but he wasn't surprised. These were just the type of Omegas he had in his pack.

Turning to Beaux, August said, "Keep an eye on things while I'm gone?"

"Sure," his Beta said, though he looked a little disappointed that he wouldn't get to go along. "Let me know if you find any more bodies." He chuckled, and August smiled at him politely, but he didn't really think it was funny. Hopefully, that girl wouldn't end up being just a body, and he could talk to her and figure out where she'd come from and why she'd been running through the woods in her human form.

The Alpha and the three Omegas quickly shifted into their wolf forms, leaving their clothes behind, and August ran behind the other three, letting them lead the way to the location where they'd found the girl. He was fairly certain there wouldn't be any clues about who she was or where she'd come from in that exact spot, but they hadn't had a chance to go further into the forest in the direction she'd come to see if there was anything else that could let them know what had happened to her. Now that she was safely in the Healing Center, they'd be able to do that.

It took about a half an hour for them to come upon the spot where the girl had been lying. All three of the Omegas came to a stop to let August check it out. He stood back for a moment, making a survey of what lay before him. Blood on the leaves, a rock with a dark stain of crimson on it where it looked like maybe she'd hit her head when she'd fallen, and bloody footsteps leading up to the place where she had collapsed let him know that she'd been in an awful state when they'd come across her.

"This is where she was lying," Grant said, using the mind-link, as if he hadn't figured that out.

"Let's follow her tracks as far as we can, toward the border," August said, once he was clear there was nothing else to find here.

He led the way this time, Sidney behind him, Grant and Ronnie on the other side of the trail. It was basically a straight path through the forest, heading in the direction of the border they shared with Black Hole Moon. They came to a small stream that was still on their property, and August leapt across it first, followed by his packmates. On the other side, he didn't immediately see footsteps.

"The two of you go that way," he said to the males. "Sid and I will have a look down here."

Ronnie and Grant ran off, and he headed south along the bank of the stream.

They trotted along the babbling body of water for about ten minutes before August found her entry point. He could see where she'd gotten into the water here, but her tracks weren't the only fresh ones. There were wolf tracks, too, several sets of them. Either she hadn't been alone--or she'd been followed.

Sidney leapt back across the stream and said, "The wolf tracks pick up here!"

August jumped over as well, and sure enough, there they were. The two of them followed the tracks for a few minutes but then, they disappeared, short of where the girl had gotten out of the water. On the other side of the stream, August could see the wolf prints on the other side, disappearing into the thick forest headed toward Black Hole lands. He hadn't noticed them before because they weren't running parallel to the stream, and he had been looking for human prints, not wolves. So, whoever had followed her had given up and headed back home, probably thinking she'd drowned. The stream was narrow, but it was deep in places and had a rushing current.

If he knew the Omegas of Black Hole, though, he had a feeling they wouldn't give up. Whoever this girl was that they had been chasing her down, they would want confirmation that she was dead, or they'd want her returned to them. If it was up to August, they'd get neither. Clearly, she had been abused by someone, and he wanted to know why. Unless there was a damn good reason, and he couldn't think of what that could possibly be, they'd have some justice coming their way for leaving her nearly beaten to death and lying in the forest alone to die.

CHAPTER 4 CHECKING IN

August was torn. Part of him wanted to immediately run straight to Black Hole Pack's Alpha and ask him what he knew about the woman, but he remembered what Sidney had said in the Healing Center and thought that probably wasn't the best idea. The other part of him wanted to sprint back to the Healing Center and check on the woman. He had to make sure that she was still alive. Even though he'd just gotten a glimpse of her tiny frame, something about her was intriguing in a way he'd never experienced before. Seeing all that she'd been through, how far she'd run, how much blood she'd spilled, all to get away from something so awful she was willing to run into the unknown to flee it, had his heart pounding out of his chest as he made his way back to the village, wanting to see how she was doing.

The other three wolves went on their way to finish their patrol, and August came back into town by himself, letting Beaux know he was back so that his Beta could go on about his business. Only stopping to put his clothes back on, August rushed past pack members who wanted to know what was going on, while quickly assuring them that everything was under control. He reached the Healing Center and braced himself for a second before pushing into the door, his need to know how she was stomping out the fear that maybe she wasn't okay.

The curtain was closed in front of the bed, but he could sense his mother was still back there, so he stepped over and pulled it open without thinking.

"August!" his mother shouted, pulling a sheet over the naked girl. August had hardly seen anything at all since he had been looking at where he expected his mother to be standing, but he quickly backed away, pulling the curtain closed as his mother continued to shout. "I'm getting her cleaned up! What are you thinking?"

"I'm sorry, Mom! I'm sorry!" he said, feeling his face turning bright red. For a moment he was actually happy the girl was still unconscious or else this would be embarrassing for both of them, instead of just him, even though he had truly seen very little. What he had seen of her petite body was covered in bruises, cuts, and dirt. His mother clearly had just started cleaning her up.

Staying outside of the curtain, August took a deep breath and asked his mother, "How is she?"

"She's doing better, now that I have an IV started and am giving her some medicine and fluids," Isabella said. "I think she's going to pull through, but it may take another day or two for her to come around."

"You do think she will, though?" August asked, standing outside of the curtain with his hands on his hips.

His mother pulled the curtain open slightly and stepped out to speak to him. Nodding, she said, "I believe so, but it's hard to say. I'm not sure why she's unconscious now. While she does have a small gash in her head, I don't think it's enough to knock a person out. So it could be exhaustion or it could be the strain of whatever she was running from."

August took a deep breath and ran his hand along his jaw, thinking. "It looks like she came from Black Hole. She was being pursued, though it looks like they lost her at the stream and went back."

"Have you got patrols out?" Isabella asked, her face mirroring his concern.

"Yes." He considered saying more about where he'd sent his Omegas, but he knew he didn't need to. "There was a lot of blood, Mom."

"I can see that, judging by the shape she's in, especially her feet."

"It just doesn't make any sense. Why didn't she shift?"

"I don't know," Isabella admitted. She patted August on the shoulder. "Hopefully, she'll wake up in a day or two, and she'll be able to answer all of our questions. In the meantime, all we can do is protect our borders, keep treating her, and pray to the Moon Goddess for her strength and wisdom."

August nodded in agreement, though the last of those options wasn't something he did quite as often as his mom. Still, thinking about the petite woman lying on the bed behind the curtain, he did say a quick prayer to the Moon Goddess, knowing it couldn't hurt. He needed her to wake up so he could figure out what was going on, but beyond that, he just needed her to be okay for reasons he couldn't quite put a finger on, but he felt them just the same.

CHAPTER 5 FOREIGN

Voices she did not recognize met her ears well before her eyes would cooperate. She couldn't quite make out what they were saying, but she knew there were people nearby, at least two of them. One sounded like a woman, kind and caring, something she didn't have a lot of experience with. The other was a younger person. Maybe a child. Or a teenaged girl? As her mind began to clear, the words became easier to understand.

"Let her rest, and hopefully, she'll be able to tell us something soon," the older woman was saying.

"I'll change her bandages again in an hour or so," said the other.

Her eyes flickered open, finally, and a bright light filtered through her eyelashes. She wasn't sure, but this place seemed unfamiliar. But then... everything seemed unfamiliar. Her body didn't hurt anymore, so that was something. Still, wherever her eyes landed, strangeness surrounded her in a way that made her heart rate increase.

It was then that the older woman, who was standing at the foot of the bed next to a younger lady, looked over and saw her. "Hi there," she said in a gentle voice. "Are you awake?"

She nodded her head slowly. The woman looked friendly. She had graying brown hair and was wearing a white jacket over her blue and yellow flowered dress. The other girl was wearing an odd outfit of large blue pants and a matching shirt with a V collar. Her dirty blonde hair was in a messy bun on the top of her head, but she had a smile on her face as well.

The older woman took a few steps closer, and that was scary. She couldn't help but shirk back a little, her knees bending.

"It's okay," she said with her hands up so that it was easy to see they were empty. "We're not going to hurt you. We're here to help." Her smile was warm and friendly. "I'm Isabella, and this is my assistant, Cleo."

"HI," Cleo said with a friendly wave. She was still standing at the end of the bed.

"Are you feeling all right? You've got some pain medicine in that IV, but if I need to adjust it, I'm happy to."

Her eyes went to the bag of fluids hanging beside her, and then she realized there was a tube stuck in her arm. Her first instinct was to pull it out, but it didn't hurt, and if it had medicine in it, then maybe this was a good thing, even though it was frightening.

Isabella took another step closer and asked, "Do you remember what happened to you?"

It should've been an easy question, but she had no idea what she was talking about. All she could remember was fear and pain. Running, falling, knowing someone was behind her. She had no idea where she had been running from or why. The thought of it had her heart leaping into her throat again.

"Take some deep breaths," Isabella said. "We don't have to talk about it right now, if you don't want to. Are you hungry?"

She nodded. That was something she was sure of. She was definitely hungry.

"Cleo, why don't you go get our new friend some soup and some fruit?"

"Sure thing, Luna Isabella," Cleo said. She was still smiling when she stepped away.

There was something familiar about that word, Luna, and she didn't like it, though she couldn't remember why. She took a deep breath, hoping Cleo hurried back with the food. Her stomach was rumbling.

"We'll get some food in you, and then you can rest some more." Isabella had a kind, patient smile, and it made her feel better. "I just have one quick question for you, sweetheart."

"Wh--what?" Her voice was weak and gravely and sounded foreign to her. Maybe that was the way it always sounded.

With that reassuring smile on her face, Isabella asked, "What's your name, dear?"

It should've been easy, automatic, tip-of-the-tongue don't think about it. But... when she opened her mouth, nothing came out. "Uh... I don't know," she admitted.

Isabella's eyebrows raised. "You don't know your name, honey?"

She shook her head. "No, I don't know... anything."

CHAPTER 6 MERCY

"You don't remember anything?" Isabella asked, looking at the girl with an expression of both worry and sadness in her eyes.

She lifted a hand to her hair again and noted that it seemed odd that it was so short. Hadn't she had longer hair? "Uh, no. I don't remember much of anything. Just…." What did she remember? Flashes of memories flickered through her mind as she thought about what she had been through recently. "Running." She saw faces, angry ones. Long, sharp teeth. Hands raised and flying in her direction. She remembered the pain, too. Her bones ached. Her feet had been bleeding. She'd remembered urging herself to keep going, to move on as fast as she could go. She just couldn't remember… why.

Isabella sat down on the edge of her bed, next to her knee. "Do you remember anything else, honey?"

She closed her eyes, trying to pull something out of the darkness. Her mind felt heavy, like a sponge that had sat so long in a pool of water that it had soaked up everything around it, locking it away where it couldn't be found again. All she saw were flashes, and each one of them contained an image that made her tremble. Whatever it was she was meant to remember, she didn't think she wanted to.

Slowly, she shook her head, opening her eyes. A tear slid down her cheek. "I'm sorry. I can't remember anything."

Isabella lifted her hand, and she immediately flinched away, causing the older woman to slowly lower her hand. "Oh, honey, I was just going to wipe the tear off of your cheek. I'm sorry. I didn't mean to frighten you."

"It's okay," she said, feeling a rush of color flood her face. She swiped at the tear herself.

"Whatever you've been through, it must've been pretty terrible, sweetheart."

A nod and a hard swallow was all she could muster as she stared at her folded, scratched up hands in her lap. No words would come to mind, so she didn't bother to respond.

"Well, you're here now, and you're safe," Isabella reminded her, patting her on the leg through the thin, whit blanket. "You can stay here as long as you like, dear."

"Thank you." It was a soft whisper. Anything else would've choked in her throat.

"Of course, honey. Think nothing of it. We are just glad you're here and safe." Isabella patted her again and let out a small chuckle. "Mercy, though, we'll have to think of something to call you, sweetheart. We can't keep calling you, 'the girl,' now can we? That just won't do."

"Mercy?" she repeated, thinking about what that word meant.

"Oh, it's just an old saying, something my grandma used to say," Isabella explained, as if she had been asking why she'd said the word.

She knew what mercy meant. She also knew what it meant not to have mercy, though she couldn't remember exactly who had been unmerciful. "Mercy," she repeated. "I think… that's what you've given me. Mercy."

"Mercy?" Isabella repeated, suddenly realizing what the girl was saying. "That would make a lovely name. Mercy."

She took a deep breath and settled back a little bit into the thick pillows. Perhaps she had been someone in the past who didn't deserve mercy, or couldn't get it, but now, looking around this room, at the care that had been provided for her, at the warm face of the woman sitting next to her, she had a feeling mercy was exactly what she had been granted. "Yes, I think so, too," she said.

"All right then, Mercy. I will go let the Alpha know that you're awake."

That word--Alpha--struck fear in her heart. Mercy's eyes widened, and her lip began to quiver. "Why?" she asked.

"So he can meet you."

She took a deep breath and tried to still her pounding heart. Whatever it was about that word, she didn't like it. She had to trust Isabella, though. If she wanted her to meet this Alpha, he must be the type of person who would show her kindness, or else, she hadn't found any mercy at all.

CHAPTER 7 INTRODUCTIONS

August

August pushed through the door of the Health Center, coming as soon as his mother had let him know that the girl was awake and talking. He'd been in such a rush to get over to see her, he hadn't let Isabella tell him much. For some reason he couldn't explain, the urge to see her for himself had compelled him to hang up the phone and jump up from his desk. Now, he did his best to slow his steps as he walked into the room, trying not to look like he was in such a rush, even though his heart was hammering in his chest.

The curtain around the bed was pulled back so that as soon as he stepped through the door, his eyes met the large blue ones staring at him from across the room. Her black hair stuck out around her pale face, and an inquisitive expression let him know she wasn't sure what to think of him. His mother was standing at the foot of the bed, a smile on her face.

Words lodged in his throat as he wasn't sure who to speak to first or what to say. The girl set a bowl and spoon she'd been holding on a tray next to the bed, the spoon clattering against the glass bowl as her hand quivered slightly. Was she… frightened? Of him?

"August," his mother said. "Thanks for coming over."

"Of course," he said, glad that his voice didn't expose the raw feelings that were churning inside of him. Whatever it was about this girl that had him all worked up, he couldn't say, but it was uncomfortable in the same way swallowing a large pill as a child had been. Even though he didn't particularly like it, he knew it was for the best.

"Mercy, dear, this is my son. August."

"H-hi," she said as he took a few steps over toward the bed.

August was about to say he was glad to meet her when his mother added, "The Alpha."

Immediately, the girl's posture changed. Despite the IV in her arm and the blanket on her lap, she swiftly moved into a crouching position on the bed, her knees bent beneath her slender form, and her head touching the bed, as if it were the floor and she was cowering before him.

His mom reacted more quickly than he did. "Oh, honey, you don't need to do that," she assured the girl, helping her back beneath the blanket and checking the IV. "Sweetheart, please be careful. We don't need to pull this loose."

"I'm… sorry," she said, her eyes flickering from his mother to him. "It's just… you said Alpha. Aren't Alphas revered?"

August let a nervous chuckle slip from between his lips. "Not like that," he said, approaching her bed. She didn't move this time, but then, his mother still had a hand on her shoulder. August extended his hand. "Hi. It's nice to meet you. What's your name?" He thought his mother had called her something, but he wasn't sure.

"I don't know," she said, her tiny hand touching his, sending a spark of electricity all the way to his elbow.

"You don't know?" he asked, puzzled.

She shook her head as she released his hand, leaving his palm cold. "I don't remember."

"August, she doesn't remember anything," his mother explained.

His eyes widened slightly but then he caught himself and lowered his eyebrows. No need to make a big deal out of it. "That's okay," he said with a shrug. "It's probably temporary."

His mother agreed. "I'm sure it is. We've decided to call her Mercy." She smiled at the girl, and the corners of her mouth upturned slightly in response. Isabella picked up the bowl which contained just a small amount of soup in the bottom and patted Mercy's shoulder. "I'll let you two talk."

August waited for his mom to walk out of the room before the awkward silence that invaded the space overcame him, compelling him to talk. He cleared his throat and asked, "How are you?"

"Fine," she said, not meeting his eyes. "Thank you."

She was clearly terrified of him, and he had no idea why that would be. But then, if she didn't remember anything, he might never find out. All of the questions he'd been preparing to ask her since she'd been brought in were pointless now. Where had she come from? Why was she running? Was she safe? Did she want to go back or was there somewhere else they could take her? Hell, she didn't even know the basic, first question he wanted to ask--what was her name?

"How are you feeling?" He realized as soon as the words came out of his mouth it was essentially the same question he'd already asked. He tried to hide the embarrassment that threatened to redden his face.

"I'm okay." At least she hadn't said the same thing in response to the similar question as she'd said before. "Tired."

"Oh," he said, assuming that meant she wanted to go to sleep. "Well, I won't keep you up."

"No, it's fine!" she said, looking a little embarrassed herself. "I didn't mean…. It's fine."

"Okay, well, uh, you can stay here as long as you need to. I mean not here--in the Health Center. Well, you can stay here. But I meant in the pack." August rubbed the back of his neck. Why in the world did he sound like a tongue-tied prepubescent boy who'd never spoken to a girl before? This should be easy for him! He talked to pretty girls all the time.

Did he think she was pretty? She was unusual looking, and her hair didn't look natural. But yes, she was pretty. More than that, there was just something about her that made him want to protect her from the world.

"Thank you," she said, her smile wider than before. "I appreciate your hospitality, Alpha August."

The way her lips formed his name made it sound sweeter than it ever had before. Again, his face threatened to turn red. "Of course," he said. "I'll let you get some rest now."

"All right," she said, looking up at him between her eyelashes before dropping her eyes again. "Thanks."

"Have a good night." He gave her an awkward wave and then headed for the door, knowing he was going to go back over this conversation a million times and kick himself for sounding like a big dork.

Maybe when she woke up again, she wouldn't remember how silly he'd sounded during their first conversation. Did amnesia work that way? He didn't think so.

As he walked back toward his office, one thing was for sure: he was never going to forget Mercy.

CHAPTER 8 AWAKE

Mercy

The ceiling above her bed was painted bright white, and with the moonlight filtering in through the small window above the door, one that wasn't covered with curtains, it reflected the light, giving Mercy something to stare at as she lay on her back, alone with her thoughts.

She had met the Alpha. August, that was his name. He was handsome and strong, and the moment she saw him, she felt at peace and safe. Well, that wasn't entirely true. When she'd first met him, she'd heard that word--Alpha--and immediately flipped out. What had caused her to react that way, she wasn't sure, but there was clearly something buried deep in her mind that made her fear the Alpha.

She hadn't reacted that way when she'd learned that Isabella was the Luna of this pack, but then, she'd known Isabella was kind before she knew her station. Mercy had to wonder how she might've reacted if she had heard she was in the presence of the Luna before she knew Isabella was so kind.

Her arm was a little sore where the IV had been, but Isabella had removed it before she left. Tucking it beneath the pillow, Mercy stared up at the shadow of a tree branch that flickered across the ceiling. The branch brought images of the forest, of her run, and the fear she'd been feeling inside of her. Not a trace of where she'd been before she started tearing through the forest came to mind, nothing but images so unrecognizable, they were akin to the shadow before her eyes now. None of the pictures in her mind seemed real; they were just representations of something else, something with substance. But she had no idea what those things were.

Mercy's eyes grew heavy. She blinked a few times and considered trying to go back to sleep. She was afraid to do that, though, because something told her that her mind was full of memories that would show up as soon as she allowed herself to slip out of the conscious realm. What if there were nightmares she couldn't wake from? Or what if whomever she'd been running from came for her while she slept?

Luna Isabella had assured her that their pack was patrolling with extra numbers that night. Likewise, there was a code on the door that kept it locked at night for everyone who didn't know the six digits to pop it open. Presently, the only ones who knew the code were her, Alpha August, and Cleo. That knowledge made Mercy feel slightly safer, but she still didn't want to close her eyes.

While it made sense that the real threats of the world, the ones she'd been running from, were more dangerous than the memories threatening to burst through as soon as she reached the dream world, she was more afraid of sleeping than she was of being recaptured presently.

Recaptured. That seemed like an odd way for her subconscious to think about it. Didn't that imply that she had been captured before? Was that why she was running? Mercy sighed and readjusted on the pillow, smoothing the blanket with the hand that wasn't beneath the pillow. She couldn't remember the answer to that question, of course, but she knew, wherever she had been, it was bad.

But this place… this place was good. She had the feeling she hadn't been this comfortable in a long time. She had been starving, and Isabella told her she'd been dehydrated as well. She had bruises, cuts, and bone breaks in various stages of healing all over her body. Whatever had happened to her, it had to have been monstrous.

The idea of being there again, in a few moments, when she fell asleep, was unappealing.

Yet, Mercy's eyes were heavy, and she was losing the battle of staying awake. As she began to drift off, a voice filled her mind. "Get down! Now! On your knees, bitch!" a woman shouted. She knew it wasn't real, that it was a memory taking shape in her dreams, but even as she was sleeping, a tear trickled down her cheek, and Mercy began to cry.

CHAPTER 9 SOCIAL

August

Sitting alone in his office until late in the night, August did some research on surrounding packs, which was difficult because most of the Alphas and their families didn't post their business on social media for everyone in the world to see. For the most part, shifters tended to keep to themselves, completely cut off from the human world. That being said, there were some younger members of the packs who kept up on that sort of thing. It was a crime punishable by death to post any information to the outside world about the existence of shifters, so no one would be foolish enough to post anything about what they were, but some of the teens and young adults posted pictures of themselves and their friends on social media apps.

August turned his computer on and flipped through a few of the apps, looking for pictures that were readily accessible to anyone. Some of them, he searched by hashtags he thought might be relevant to the youth of the surrounding packs. The rest of the world knew their villages by their pack names and thought that the people who lived there were either religious fanatics of some sort or members of a commune. While they were known to live in parts of the country that had lots of dangerous animals roaming around, no one knew that those animals were shifter wolves. Pack villages were known on the map by their pack names, so if one were to pull out a map of the place where he lived, it would simply say, "Rising Moon."

Deciding it was worth a try to search for #blackholemoon, August scanned the pictures on one app particularly popular with teens. To his surprise, lots of pictures came up. There was a girl he recognized as the sister of the Alpha in most of the pictures, and he realized this account, @sistersister must be her account. Her name was Stephanie Voles, and her brother, Rider Voles, was an asshole if August had ever met one.

Still, Stephanie seemed nice enough. She was kind of cute, but in a fake sort of way, with way too much makeup on, and an unbelievable amount of blonde highlights in her dark, wavy hair. She made all kinds of faces for the camera, including that duck bill look he thought was so ridiculous and an ungodly amount of peace signs.

August was just about ready to give up scrolling through the pictures when something in the background caught his eye. He wouldn't have even noticed if it wasn't for the posture of the person in the back corner.

Saving the picture to his desktop, he zoomed in tight on the girl in the back corner and recognized her face, even though she was crying. She was on her knees, her hands folded in front of her as she made herself as small as possible, and a man stood before her, just off to the side. He was only visible from the knees down, but in his hand, he held a whip. Her hair was long and blonde, and her face was scrunched up in agony and terror while in front of her a group of girls blew kisses to the camera like they had no idea someone was being tortured behind them.

August felt sick to his stomach and tears of rage filled his eyes. He had no idea what was going on but it looked horrific. And even though her hair was different and the picture was grainy because it was taken at a distance, he was sure. That was Mercy he was looking at.

He was going to find out what had happened to her and make that man with the whip and anyone else who had ever mistreated her pay--if it was the last thing he ever did.

CHAPTER 10 FINDERS KEEPERS

August

"Honey, I know how angry you are, and I don't blame you. I feel the same way," Isabella was saying, sitting next to August on the couch in the home they shared together. "But, baby, I have to tell you, I just don't think it's a good idea."

August was stunned to hear his mother's words. She'd already said the same thing several times since he'd shown her the pictures he'd found online. While only one of them showed Mercy, the one where she was on her knees in the background, crying, he'd printed that one off along with several others, ones that showed the faces of key players from Black Hole Moon, including the Alpha's sister, Stephanie, and the Alpha himself, Rider. His plan had been to take the pictures in to Mercy and show them to her to see if it jarred any of her memories.

Isabella clearly didn't think that was a good idea.

"Mom, she needs to remember. If she doesn't remember, we can't help her," he explained--again.

"No, dear, not right now. That's not what she needs at all. Right now, she needs to know that she's safe and cared for. If we bring back all of the bad feelings and terror she's felt before, we might lose her completely."

August sighed and ran a hand through his hair. He understood what his mother was saying, he really did, but he disagreed. He thought Mercy was stronger than that, that she was strong enough to look at these pictures and face what she'd been through. But then, he wondered if he'd want to look at the person who'd tortured him the way that Mercy clearly had been tortured. He was almost certain the man with the whip in the picture was Rider.

"All right, Mom," he finally said. "I won't show her. Not now anyway."

Isabella gave him a satisfied smile and said, "I know how much you care about her, that you want to protect her, dear. You can still do that without her remembering anything for now."

It was hard to take her directions, but he decided he'd let it go for now. "Is she awake?"

Isabella nodded. "Cleo called a bit ago. Said she was awake when she went in early this morning. I'll be headed that way now."

August had been up all night. Even though he'd laid in his bed for a few hours, he couldn't sleep. He'd been waiting to talk to his mom about what he'd found. Now, he'd interrupted her schedule, and all for nothing. Maybe she was right, and it was best not to worry Mercy over these things just yet. Maybe there was a better way to handle it.

"Do you want to go with me?" Isabella asked as she stood and walked toward the door.

Looking at the pictures he had gathered in his hand, August set them down on the coffee table and said, "Sure." He did want to see her. He was just a little afraid that something might have changed overnight. What if she couldn't remember having met them the day before? What if she was frightened of him again?

Deciding he'd just have to go find out, August followed his mother out the door and down the porch. The sun was just coming up now. He stifled a yawn, wishing he had gotten at least a few hours of sleep the night before, but he'd make do.

They were almost to the clinic when he saw his Beta, Beaux, running in his direction. "Alpha!" he shouted.

Isabella stopped alongside him, a worried expression on her face. "Go on in, Mama. I'll be there in a bit," August said, rushing off to meet Beaux. Whatever it was that had him running, it had to be important.

"Be careful," Isabella said, like she always did.

"What is it, Beaux?" August asked.

"There's a phone call for you, in your office. I answered it because the caller ID said Black Hole."

August swallowed hard. "Who is it?"

"It's Alpha Rider," he said. "Do you think he's calling about the girl?"

"Yeah, I'm pretty sure he is," August said. "And we're calling her Mercy now. She can't remember her name."

"She can't remember her name?"

August was walking swiftly toward his office now, Beaux rushing to keep up. "She can't remember anything."

"Wow. That's crazy," Beaux said.

"Please don't use that word." August gave him a stern look.

"Sorry. I didn't mean she's crazy. Just that it's hard to believe she can't remember anything, that's all."

"I know." August knew Beaux wasn't trying to be offensive. "I just don't want her to feel like there's something wrong with her because she can't remember."

He reached his office and went inside, sitting down behind his desk before he took in a deep breath and picked up the receiver. "This is August."

"Alpha August." Even Rider Vole's voice sounded weasley. "How are you?"

"Not bad, Rider. How are you?"

"Well, I'm in a bit of a predicament, August, one I hope you can help me with."

"What's that?" he asked, trying to play nonchalant.

"It seems I've lost something quite valuable, and I think you might have it."

To hear him discuss Mercy like she was a commodity made August's stomach tighten. "What would that be, Rider? You misplace your dignity again?"

Rider chuckled and ignored the insult. "No, I've misplaced a wench, one I bought fair and square, and I'd like to have her back."

"A wench?" August repeated, seeing Beaux's mouth fall open at the word. "What? Are we trapped in the Middle Ages, Rider? I assure you, I don't have your wench."

"Oh, I think you have her," Rider said. "And I assure you--I'm going to get her back. One way or another."

CHAPTER 11 SHARDS

Mercy

Mercy was glad to see Isabella. She was so kind and refreshing. She'd brought Mercy some clean clothes and made sure she was able to take a shower without any help. She'd also brought her a snack, which was great, even though Cleo had brought her a full breakfast. Mercy felt like her stomach was turning inside out, she was so hungry. Now, she was sitting on the bed, feeling comfy in a pair of sweatpants and a T-shirt. They smelled like flowers and fresh cotton and made her skin feel all soft and snuggly. There was something going on with her hair, though, and it was bothering her almost as much as the fact that she couldn't remember anything. The urge to flip her hair back over her shoulder was driving her mad, but every time she went to move it, there was nothing there.

"Would you like to watch some television?" Isabella asked, once Mercy was settled in.

'What's that?" she asked. It seemed like it was something she should've known--the way she knew what clothes, food, and showers were--but when she heard the words, she had no idea what Isabella was talking about.

"It's this box here, on the wall," she said, gesturing at a black rectangle on the wall across the room from her. She picked up another black rectangle, a much smaller one, and pushed some buttons, bringing it over to Mercy.

Immediately, a light began to glow in the box, and noises sounded, including a lot of loud laughing. Mercy wasn't sure what to make of this. People were walking around, talking to one another, not even paying any attention to her. It was like they couldn't see her at all.

"Wh-what are they doing?" she asked as Isabella brought her the small rectangle.

"Oh, it's just shows. Movies. You can watch the news. Just flip through and see if there's anything that looks interesting to you."

She put the small rectangle in Mercy's hand and showed her how to push the buttons to make different people show on the box. "You say this is called a tell vision?"

"Television," Isabella said with a smile. "Or TV. That thing in your hand is called a remote control, or just remote. You really don't think you remember this?"

Mercy shook her head. "I don't think I've ever seen it before. Does everyone have these?" She vaguely remembered seeing a different kind of rectangle in people's hands, but she thought that was called a phone. She was pretty sure she'd never seen one up close before.

A large gray animal showed up on the screen making weird noises. It was standing in tall grass with a wide blue sky behind its head. Mercy set the remote down. Whatever this thing was, it seemed fascinating to her.

She watched the animals for a long time, trying to understand what the voice man was saying, but she didn't understand a lot of it. When the door opened a bit later, she would've had trouble pulling her eyes away if it wasn't August. The second she saw him, she put the remote down and smiled at him. "Hi."

"Hi, Mercy," he said, greeting his mother and then coming over to speak to her. "How have you been?"

"I'm okay," Mercy said, thinking it was mostly true, considering. "I'm just watching tell vision."

"Oh, yeah. African elephants." He sat down in a chair near her, a smile on his face. He smelled fresh, like the rain, to Mercy, and she sort of remembered how nice it was to stand outside in a downpour, though she wasn't sure why that memory stuck out to her when nothing else did. Not that it was specific.

"I'm going to take these herbs over to Mrs. Barkley," Isabella said, picking up a bottle from her desk. "I'll be back in a bit."

"I'll keep Mercy company," August said.

Isabella gave him a look Mercy didn't know quite how to read, and August nodded, then Isabella went out the door. Thinking there was no point in asking what that was about, Mercy returned her attention to the Alpha. She knew she'd always been afraid of people with that title, though the reason was lost in the black hole of her mind. She wasn't afraid of August, though. Not even a little bit. He seemed powerful, rugged, even invincible in a way. But not scary.

"So… how are you feeling?" he asked her, the nonchalance in his voice seeming forced.

"I'm all right," she said with a nod. "My head doesn't hurt anymore."

"That's good," he said. "You have more color in your face, too, I think."

She smiled, thinking that must be a compliment.

"Mom's clothes fit you pretty well."

A giggle escaped her lips as she looked down at what she was wearing. It was a little too big, but not too bad. "It's comfortable."

"Yeah. You look great."

"Thanks."

The conversation was a bit more tedious than she would've hoped, but then, she had no idea how often she'd spoken to another person. Maybe never. Maybe that's why she was bad at it.

"Still… no memories then?"

Mercy shook her head. "Unfortunately… no. Not really. I had a few dreams, but nothing that really stuck."

He looked interested anyway. August scooted forward onto the edge of his seat. "What sort of dreams?"

Mercy really didn't want to think about it; they had been scary, and she didn't want them back in her mind. Still, he seemed so intrigued, she felt like she had to say something. "I don't know. Branches. Arms. Screaming people. Frowns…." She shook her head as she was speaking. None of it made much sense. "Just a lot of anger, I guess."

August reached over and put his hand gently on her knee. "I'm really sorry you've been through so much, Mercy. You don't have to worry about any of that anymore, though, because you're safe here."

"Thank you," she said, putting her hand on top of his.

"I'm going to make sure you never have to go back to Black Hole Moon."

Mercy's eyes widened at his words and a ripple of fear passed through her body. She had no idea what he was talking about, but those words made her want to scream. Mercy closed her eyes, her hands fisted as August got up and put his hand on her shoulder.

"Mercy? What's the matter?" he asked her.

Behind his head, the tell vision splintered into a thousand shards of glass.

CHAPTER 12 CALM

August

"Mercy? Are you all right?" The sound of the television exploding behind August was alarming, but he was more concerned about the girl in front of him. She was shaking like a leaf, her eyes closed, her face turning pale. "Mercy, please, open your eyes!"

"What's going on?" Isabella demanded as she came into the room.

August glanced at her but then returned his gaze to Mercy. "I don't know. She just…" He shook his head, not sure how to put it. He didn't want to tell his mom that this was his fault, that he'd jarred this reaction from her when he'd said Black Hole Moon, but he'd have to. Not now, though. Now, they needed to help her.

"Mercy, honey, open your eyes," Isabella said in a calm, soothing voice as she sat on the bed next to the girl, her arms fixed on Mercy's face. "Look at me. You're safe. It's me. Isabella. Look in my eyes, honey."

Slowly, Mercy's eyes opened, and she looked at Isabella.

"Good, good. Take some deep breaths. Try to calm down, sweet girl." Isabella mimicked the deep breaths she wanted Mercy to take

Mercy inhaled deeply, and slowly, she stopped shaking. Her face began to get color in it again, and her breathing returned to normal. She looked like she was regaining her composure, but just when August was about to let his guard down, he noticed a trickle of red from her ear.

"Mom, she's bleeding."

"What?" Isabella asked, not able to see it from where she was sitting.

"Her ear. It's bleeding." August reached for a tissue to wipe it away, but Isabella took it from his hand and gently dabbed it on the side of Mercy's face. Once she'd cleaned the side August could see, she did the same on the other side.

A million questions entered his mind. What in the world would cause her ears to bleed? Was she okay? Did she have an internal injury? As much as he also wanted to know what had happened to the TV, he was more concerned about how she was doing.

"There, sweetie. You're fine now. Why don't you rest some more okay?" Isabella stood up and helped Mercy lay down on the bed, being as gentle with the fragile girl as she would a wounded kitten or a newborn baby.

"I'm sorry," Mercy said as she lay down, clearly zapped of her energy after the traumatic event.

"No, no, there's nothing to be sorry about, honey. It's fine." Isabella smoothed her hair and tucked the blankets over her.

"But… the tell vision," Mercy said, her eyes focused on the place on the wall where the charred remains of the black box still hung in skeleton form.

"That old thing?" August chimed in with a smile. "It's not a big deal. We needed a new one anyway."

"You're not… m-mad, Alpha?" Her lips were trembling again, just slightly, as she asked.

August reached over and took her hand in his. "No, Mercy. Not at all. I don't think I could ever be mad at you."

Her eyes widened, and a small smile came across her face, but then it slowly faded away. "I think you could be," she said. Her tone was haunting, and it sent a shiver down August's spine.

"Nah, not me," he assured her, even though he had to wonder why she'd said what she'd said in that tone. Chalking it up to exhaustion, he squeezed her hand and then let it go, knowing he'd have to face the wrath of his mother now, and if anyone could cause an explosion that would shake him up, it was Isabella.

CHAPTER 13: PLAN

August

"What did you say to that woman?" Isabella asked as they stood outside of the healing center. "Really, August! The television exploded!"

"I know, Mother. I was there." He tried to keep his tone light because he didn't want to upset her any more than she already was. Clearly, he was good at upsetting women. "I made a mistake, all right?"

"Did you try asking her about her past? You didn't show her those damn pictures did you?"

"No, and no. Not exactly, anyway. On the first one."

"What's that now?" Isabella folded her hands beneath her bosom and waited for an answer that made sense.

August wasn't sure he had an answer that made sense. "Mom, I just said she'd never have to go back. That's all!" More or less, that was true. Did his mom really need to know where he'd said Mercy didn't need to go back to?

"That's all?" she repeated. "Are you sure about that, son? Because that doesn't seem like the sort of thing a person would say that would make a television explode. I've never seen anything like that before. And we are sure that she did it, right? That it wasn't an electrical surge of some kind?"

"Considering nothing else was affected, I'm going to have to say it had to be her. It corresponded directly with her strange behavior as well." He'd been so scared, seeing Mercy lock up like that, rocking, her eyes closed, all pale. He was so thankful his mother had arrived when she had or else Mercy might've really gotten hurt.

"Did you mention the name of the place you think she came from?" Isabella wanted to know.

She was too smart for him. He should've known she'd figure it out. Slowly, he nodded his head.

"August! What's the matter with you?" She smacked him in the bicep hard enough for it to sting. "I told you to leave her alone!"

"I'm sorry, Mom. I am! I didn't mean to. It just slipped out." He rubbed his arm and could see in his mother's face that she felt bad for hurting him. Sometimes she didn't know her own strength--like a mama grizzly bear protecting, and then assaulting, her cubs.

"You cannot say anything else about it until she's ready, okay? Seriously! You can set her back into that comatose state, and we don't need that!"

"All right, all right. I'm sorry."

"I'm sorry I hit you!"

"Me, too!"

Isabella laughed and then wrapped her arms around August. He hugged her tight and kissed her cheek. "Thank you for fixing her again, Mama."

"Of course. Just… stop breaking her, all right. I like that little girl."

"I like her, too," August admitted, though he wouldn't call her a little girl. She was tiny, but she was no girl.

"We'll need to find a bed for her in the pack house and get a couple of the girls to help watch out for her. She'll need clothes and other necessities as well. We'll have to find her a way to contribute to the pack without putting her on patrols and making sure she's safe. She's not ready to leave yet, but she will be soon enough. Hopefully."

August nodded. He'd been thinking about all of that stuff as well, but he had one idea that was a little different than his mother's suggestion. "Instead of the pack house, why don't we put her somewhere a little more comfortable, a little safer, where if someone comes poking around looking for her, she'll be safer?"

Isabella's forehead wrinkled. "Where?"

August shrugged, not sure he was ready to say what he was thinking out loud. He couldn't resist the look his mom was giving him, so he said it quickly. "I don't know. Our house?"

Her eyes widened. "Our house? Man, you really do like her."

August's face heated. "It's not like that, Mama."

"Uh, huh. Whatever. Okay. Sure. She can stay with us."

August nodded and tried to act nonchalant, but inside, his stomach was twisting in knots. Maybe it wasn't a good idea to have Mercy under his roof because he clearly was attracted to her in a way he couldn't quite describe, but he also knew he needed to protect her, and that was the best way to make sure she was safe. He had to keep her from Black Hole Moon. No matter what.

CHAPTER 14 LISTS

Mercy

The shell of the tell vision on the wall was haunting as Mercy sat in her bed, trying to figure out what had happened. Even after the mess on the floor was cleaned up, her mind wouldn't stop focusing on how she'd made the tell vision do that--and why.

Black Hole Moon--those were the words that Alpha August had said. They'd made her lose control. She didn't know why. When she tried to remember what those words meant, nothing came to mind. She wasn't even sure what a blackhole was.

She did know what the moon was, though. She didn't have a lot of memories, but she could remember a window, similar to the one near her bed now, with a large, glowing orb situated right outside of it, so large and bright... it was the only thing that made her feel calm, made her feel connected to the rest of the world.

But that was it. She couldn't even remember where that room was or why she was in it.

Cleo came in from one of the other rooms, walking slowly, as if she was afraid she might say something to make Mercy upset again and cause another explosion.

"Do you need anything, Mercy?" she asked, her voice even softer than usual. "Are you in any pain? Or are you hungry?"

"I'm fine," Mercy assured her. She turned to look at the table next to her bed and saw that she had plenty of water, too. What she really wanted was to talk to Alpha August again, to tell him that she was sorry--again. He'd said he wasn't worried about the tell vision, but she didn't think that was true. She also just wanted to see him because, despite the fact that he'd triggered whatever happened inside of her to make the tell vision explode, he had a way of making her feel at peace that she didn't feel when anyone else was around.

"All right. Well, if you need anything, I'll be over at the desk doing some paperwork. We've got some supplies to order." Cleo gave her a bright smile, and Mercy smiled back, but it was obvious Cleo was afraid of her now.

Was there anyone else here who was capable of exploding things the way that Mercy just had? The way that everyone was reacting, she had to think that she was the only one. Did anyone else have any sort of powers, other than the ability to shift into a wolf?

It was hard to believe that she was capable of doing that, but she knew that she was. She could feel her wolf form itching inside of her, wanting to get out. She didn't know why she'd been running as a human, though. It would make so much more sense for her to shift into a wolf to run. Her feet wouldn't be so cut up if she had done that. Was there something preventing her from shifting?

Her head was so full of questions, and none of them had answers. Not easy ones anyway. Would she always feel this lost and all alone? Was it possible that someday all of this would be as foggy and vague as the nightmare she'd had the night before?

Now that the tell vision was gone, Mercy had nothing more to do than sit on her bed or go to sleep. Going to sleep was tempting. She did feel awfully tired. But if she slept, she might dream, and she didn't want to do that.

What she did want to do was speak to Alpha August again. He was the Alpha of this pack, though. She knew that he had to be busy. He had an entire pack to run. She was just one small interloper who had come into his world and disturbed everything. And despite what he'd said, she still felt bad for exploding his device and scaring him with the way she reacted to what he'd said.

Black Hole Moon. Why were those words so terrifying? Were there any other words that would terrify her the way that those did? She hoped not.

She sat there for about an hour, staring at the wall across from her, thinking about everything that she couldn't remember and the few things she did remember. It seemed so weird that she knew what water was but not her own name. She knew the names of plenty of objects around the room but not how old she was or what she'd been doing the day before--before she started to run.

Mercy made a mental list of all of the things she could remember. It was short. She also made a mental list of all of the things she wanted to know. That list was much longer. She wished she had some paper and a pen to write them down, but she didn't want to bother Cleo for that, not when she could keep them in her mind. After all, there wasn't much else in her head to take up space.

Her stomach was beginning to rumble. For some reason, Mercy thought this was ordinary, something she was used to--being hungry. Her body was so small and frail compared to the others she'd seen. Cleo and Isabella were not large women at all, but they had muscle on their limbs. They had hips and chests. Compared to them, Mercy felt tiny--scrawny. Had she not had enough to eat?

As if he was reading her mind, Alpha August walked into the Healing Center carrying a box that smelled absolutely delicious. She had no idea what it was, but she was looking forward to finding out. She knew it had to be food--she just hoped it was for her.

With a wide smile on his face, August said, "Hi, Mercy. I thought you might be hungry. Do you like pizza?"

"I don't know," she said. "But I like the way it smells."

His smile widened. "Everyone likes pizza."

"Well, then, I guess I do, too," she said, thinking she had to be right since the smell was making her mouth water. But then… that could've been because of the man who was carrying the box just as much as it was for what was in the box.

She thought of two more questions to add to her list--"Do I like the taste of pizza?" and "Why do I want to taste the Alpha?"

CHAPTER 15 PIZZA

August

The look on Mercy's face before she'd turned to acknowledge him was haunting. August wasn't sure what to make of it. She was just staring at the wall, as if she was watching television, but since he hadn't replaced the broken one yet, that wasn't what was happening.

What was she looking at?

When she turned to acknowledge him, the vacant look faded, and a smile came to her lips. She was so beautiful. He couldn't imagine why anyone would ever want to hurt her.

Sitting the pizza on the tray next to her bed, he went to the supply closet and got a couple of paper plates and napkins. He almost asked her if she wanted a soda, but then he realized she wouldn't know what that was. "I've got a couple of cans of Coke in the refrigerator. Do you want to try that, or would you rather just have water?"

"Coke?" Mercy repeated. "What is that?"

"Tell you what. You can try it. If you don't like it, no big deal. Okay?"

She nodded, and he went into the other room to grab the drinks. When he came back, she had her eyes closed and was inhaling the scent of the pizza. "You can help yourself," he told her, bringing the cans over and pulling up a chair.

"I'll wait for you," Mercy said. It was clear she was afraid to open the box, like she didn't even know how to open it.

Setting everything else he had in his hands aside, August opened the pizza box. "We don't have a lot of restaurants in the village, but Tony's Pizza Parlor knows how to make a mean pizza pie. I hope you like pepperoni." He pulled a slice out of the box and put it on a plate for her.

Mercy took it, but she looked confused as to what to do with it. August put a slice on his own plate, opened the Cokes and sat down. He showed her how to lift the pizza to her mouth and eat it.

Mercy picked the pizza up, but the pointy end kept falling away from her mouth. August tried not to laugh as she dipped her head and finally captured it. She took a bite, and her eyes went wide.

"Do you like it?" he asked her.

"This is delicious!" Mercy said, still chewing. She took another bite. "I don't think I've ever had this before. I think I'd remember it if I did."

August chuckled, glad to see her so happy. He took a sip of his Coke and then said, "When you're ready, try the soda."

Mercy ate the entire slice of pizza before she wiped her hands on a napkin and picked up the Coke can. She held it to her nose and inhaled. A few of the bubbles went up her nose, and she pulled back. "I don't know about this." She ran her hand under her nose.

"Well, you're not supposed to inhale it, silly."

Carefully, Mercy held the can to her lips and took a sip. She did not react the same way this time as she had with the pizza, but she also didn't lower the can until she'd taken a pretty long drink.

"What do you think?" August asked her.

"It burns a little," she said. "But I like it. It's sweet and a little sour."

"I try not to drink too much of it because it has a lot of sugar, but it goes pretty well with pizza. Not as good as beer, but I figured you shouldn't have any alcohol with the medicine you've been taking."

"What's that?" Mercy asked as he dished her up another slice of pizza.

"What's beer?" he asked. She nodded. "Oh, uh, it's just another drink. But it has alcohol in it."

"What's alcohol?" She took a bite and looked at him as if the question was something anyone might ask.

"It's… well, it's a drug, I guess. A legal one. One that sometimes makes people do stupid things, but it also makes a person feel good. For a while."

"Huh," Mercy said, halfway through her pizza. "I don't know what to think about that."

"I can't blame you there." She was eating so fast, he was a little worried. "You might want to slow down. You don't want to make yourself sick."

"Can pizza make you sick?" Mercy asked, setting what was left of her slice down.

"If you eat it too fast, anything can make you sick." August replied.

Mercy picked her slice back up and took another bite, but she slowed down this time.

Once they were finished eating, August cleaned up. There were only two slices left, so he put them in the refrigerator. Cold pizza could be a whole new experience for her. He came back to her bedside and sat down.

Mercy was leaning back with one hand on her stomach. She looked full but happy. "There's something else I wanted to talk to you about, Mercy," August said, afraid he might frighten her again.

"What is it?" she asked.

He took a deep breath and blew it out slowly. "Try not to get too worked up because it's just a question, and you don't have to do anything."

She laced her fingers together, and he could see that she was starting to get anxious. The last thing he wanted to do was to make her freak out again. He'd been so scared the last time. He didn't think he could handle seeing her do that again.

"What is it?" she asked.

"Well, when you're healthy enough to leave the hospital... my mom and I have been talking and... we'd like it if you'd come and stay with us for a while. In our house."

"Stay... in the Alpha's house?" Mercy asked. August nodded.

Mercy's eyes rolled back into her head, and she fell backward, limp, onto the pillow.

"Shit."

CHAPTER 16: SAFE AND HAPPY

Mercy

THE ALPHA'S HOUSE. STAYING IN THE ALPHA'S HOUSE.... SOMETHING about those words made Mercy feel lightheaded and sick to her stomach. She couldn't help it. There was a memory there, a bad one, one she couldn't handle. Just the words coming out of August's mouth made her want to get up and run out of the room.

"Mercy!"

She heard August's voice calling her name, but all she could see was darkness, and a bit of light at the top of her eyes as they rolled back into her head.

"Mercy... Mercy! Breathe!"

At his command, oxygen filled her lungs again, and Mercy felt that she was regaining control of her body. She tried to sit back up, but she couldn't. Her eyes opened, and she saw August leaning over her, a concerned look on his handsome face.

"Are you okay?" he asked, his hand on the side of her face. "Can you hear me?"

"Yeah, yes," she said, reaching up and putting her hand on top of his. She didn't want him to move away. Having his hand on her face made her feel anchored to reality in a way she couldn't quite explain.

"I'm so sorry," August said, his voice almost a whisper. "I don't know why I keep saying things to you that make you have these sorts of reactions."

"It's not your fault," she told him, still touching his hand even though he was trying to pull it away. Instead of letting go of her completely, he interlaced his fingers with hers and moved his hand down to her side. "I don't know why it keeps happening either, but I know it's not you."

"You don't do that when my mom or Cleo are in here," he reasoned.

"True. But.. you said something about the Alpha's house, and that made me panic for some reason. I know I have a bad memory about the Alpha's house. I just don't know what it is."

She could tell that her words had upset him. His face fell, and he set his jaw in frustration. She wanted to reach up and touch his face, to feel that stubble scrape against her palm, but she didn't dare.

"I think something bad happened to you in your old pack, Mercy, but you're here now, and I promise you, nothing bad is ever going to happen to you again. I won't let that happen."

"How do you know?" She couldn't help but ask. Even though she knew that he wanted to help her, he wanted to protect her, it didn't seem possible that he could guarantee to her that she would be safe from now on.

"I know because… I won't let anything happen to you, Mercy. You're safe here. No one is going to be able to get into my pack lands and hurt you, and I'm never going to let you leave with anyone who could possibly hurt you or let you get hurt. As long as you stay here, you're safe. I promise."

Looking into his eyes, she could see that she could trust him, that he meant every word of what he was saying. Mercy felt a tear slip from her eye. August reached up and brushed it away. The feel of his fingertips on her skin sent a tingle of electricity through her, radiating down to her core.

"Thank you, Alpha," she said.

"You don't have to call me that, Mercy. You can just call me August."

"But you're the Alpha," she reminded him.

"If being the Alpha makes you afraid of me, we'll just pretend that's not who I am."

She couldn't help but smile at him. He was trying so hard. "Thank you, August."

His smile set her at ease, more so than anything else had since she'd arrived in his pack. "You're welcome, Mercy. I'll do anything I can to make sure you're not only safe here, but happy."

Mercy liked the sound of that. She was pretty sure she'd never been either of those two things before. She was already beginning to feel safe. She was looking forward to feeling happy.

CHAPTER 17 SLEEPLESS NIGHT

August

Lying in his bed that night, August stared up at the ceiling, wondering what it was going to take for him to figure out a way to talk to Mercy to keep her from freaking out every time he opened his mouth. He felt so terrible for upsetting her like that. But… this time he'd had no idea that just the question of whether or not she'd want to move in with him and his mom would make her react that way.

At least she hadn't had the same reaction as she had the time before, when he'd mentioned Black Hole Moon. He'd been able to talk her back out of this reaction much better. Whether or not it was a true sign of progress, he wasn't sure, but he'd take what he could get.

It was past midnight. He'd been lying there for a few hours, and so far, he hadn't even started to feel drowsy. He considered getting up and doing something else, maybe going for a run to tire himself out, but he didn't want to be too far away from Mercy just in case something happened. He knew he had some of his best Omegas on patrol right now, so if anyone from Black Hole Moon or any other packs came onto his territory, he'd know it right away.

And they'd be pushed back off of his property immediately.

So why was he still awake?

It was her. He couldn't stop thinking about her. She had the most beautiful face. Her eyes were so sparkly, and her hair, even though it had been hacked off and dyed, was soft and silky. She was so dainty and petite, he felt like he could just wrap his arms around her and keep her safe forever.

In order for that to work, he'd have to figure out a way to speak to her without having her break into a panic attack every time he opened his mouth. He knew it would likely take time for him to convince her that she was safe, and that he only wanted what was best for her, but he wasn't sure how long he could be patient.

All he wanted to do was touch her, hold her, kiss her….

August rolled over and tucked an arm beneath his pillow, pulling his gray-blue comforter up over his arm and tucking it beneath his chin, even though he wasn't cold. His mom used to tuck him in when he was little and probably still would if he'd let her. He knew she'd been having trouble sleeping since Mercy arrived, too. His mom felt responsible for her, too.

August closed his eyes and tried to reach for sleep, but instead, he saw Mercy's face. He didn't see her in the hospital, or even in that awful picture. Rather, he saw her standing in a field full of flowers, the sunlight making her eyes sparkle, and her hair glisten. But it wasn't that dark black color, either. It was a light blonde shade, similar to the roots that were beginning to show. It was still short, and when the wind blew, it danced around her shoulders.

She was laughing, and even though he couldn't hear it, he knew it was melodious, like a small bell ringing. He imagined she smelled more fragrant than the flowers, too. Her dress was a blue sundress with pink and white flowers, just as dainty and lovely as she was.

August opened his eyes, and the image faded. It was a lovely thought, the sort of thought that warmed his heart and made him feel like Mercy would get the happiness and joy she deserved. He would do anything he could to help her get that.

Unable to sleep, he decided to get out of bed and wander downstairs for a snack. He wasn't really hungry, but sometimes eating a little something could help him fall asleep better than just lying in bed.

When he arrived in the kitchen, he was surprised to see the light above the sink on, its dim light hardly illuminating the space at all. His mom was sitting at the island on a barstool, eating a cookie, her tea cup still steaming.

"You couldn't sleep either, huh?" he said, chuckling softly. He patted his mom on the shoulder as he went to the refrigerator to see what he might want to eat.

"No, not at all," Isabella said. "I just keep thinking about that poor girl. I can't imagine what has happened to her, where she's come from, and… how she's able to do… what she's able to do."

August rifled around in the refrigerator for a moment before deciding on a bagel. Carbs might make him sleepy. "We've seen shifters with talents before," he reminded her.

"Yes, that's true, we have. But they're nothing like this. An even keener sense of smell, even faster running, even some with healing abilities. But this… this is unusual."

August heated his bagel in the toaster. "Well, it'll be difficult to figure anything out until she remembers it, and we can hardly go asking around other packs without making people suspicious."

"I know," his mom said. "Maybe I could do some research in the library."

"The library?" August hadn't stepped foot in the library in years, not since he'd graduated from college. "Why not online?"

His mom waved him off with her wrist. "I don't know anything about that, but I know how to use the Dewey Decimal System."

Laughing, August retrieved his bagel from the machine and put some cream cheese on it. "I'm sure you do. What sort of books might you be looking for, Mom?"

"I don't know, but I'll start in the historical section, maybe some in folklore."

August nodded, thinking that made sense. "Let me know if you need any help, Mom."

"Thanks. I'm sure you have plenty of other things to keep you busy." She got up from her stool and walked over to him, kissing his cheek. "Try to get some sleep. We won't be any use to anyone if we're exhausted."

"I'll try," August promised her between bites. "'Night, Mom. I love you."

"Goodnight, dear. I love you, too."

Isabella headed upstairs, and August stared into the distance, not really seeing anything, finishing his bagel and wondering if Mercy was asleep or if she was also lying awake. If she was… what was she thinking about? Was there any chance she was thinking about him?

CHAPTER 18 LIKE CHINA

Mercy

"Well, all of your scans look normal," Luna Isabella was saying as she stood next to Mercy's bed, a bunch of papers in her hand. "We've run a lot of tests, and I don't see anything wrong, other than you're a little malnourished, but that shouldn't be causing your memory issues. I think it's safe to say it's psychological at this point, honey."

Mercy nodded, thinking she had to be right. "What do we do about that?" She wasn't sure she wanted to hear the answer.

"Well, I suppose you've got a good reason for not wanting to remember these things, honey, or else you wouldn't be blocking them all out, right?" Isabella gave her a sympathetic smile.

Not knowing what to say, Mercy let her eyes drift to the ground. Isabella had a point. Mercy knew from her dreams and from the incidents she'd had whenever August had said certain things that began to trigger those memories her mind was fighting so hard to lock away.

"We don't have a therapist or psychologist in the pack, but I believe there is one in Sunshine pack."

"Where is Sunshine pack?" Mercy asked. The idea that she might have to leave almost made her panic.

"It's a few hundred miles from here. But if she has time to work with you, we can do all of the sessions virtually. That seems to work fairly well, from what I've read in my research." Isabella gave her a reassuring smile.

"Virtually?" Mercy wasn't sure she knew what that word meant, not in that context anyway. Sometimes, she felt virtually lost--but she didn't think that was the same use of the word as what Isabella was saying now.

"Yes, it means over the Internet, essentially. On the phone, the computer, or something of that nature. Don't worry. It's not difficult. If an old lady like me can learn how to use technology for these sorts of things, I'm quite certain a young lady like yourself can do so as well. If not, I know we have plenty of pack members who'd be willing to help."

That idea made Mercy relax into her pillow a bit. It was the most at ease she'd felt in the last few days, since she'd arrived here. The thought that it might be Alpha August who was helping her also made excitement bubble up inside of her. She'd seen him a few more times in the last few days, but he hadn't stayed well. She imagined he was busy attending to all of the responsibilities he had as Alpha.

She'd gotten a little more used to accepting the fact that she didn't need to fear the Alpha here. It seemed clear that many of the memories Isabella was telling her she was trying to keep buried in her mind. Even thinking about the possibility of trying to remember them made her stomach tighten up and her head feel light and fuzzy, like she might pass out again. Since she didn't want to do that, she just pushed those thoughts aside.

"Now, let me ask you this, dear." Isabella sat down on the bed near Mercy's knees. She took a deep breath, and it was clear to Mercy that she was choosing her words very carefully. Mercy hated that everyone felt like they had to treat her like she was so fragile that she might fracture into a thousand pieces at any moment like glass dropped to the floor--or a telle vision screen.

"What is it?" Mercy asked, trying to seem like she knew for a fact she wouldn't freak out, no matter what Isabelle asked.

"Well, how would you feel about… coming home… to our house… in a day or two." Isabelle looked at her with wide eyes, a mother watching a child carry antique chinaware to the sink over concrete.…

Mercy already knew there'd been talk of her leaving the medical facility to move into the Alpha's house. When she thought about it that way, it did make her heart rate increase. But when she considered that she was moving in with Alpha August and Luna Isabella… that was different. That sounded like a lovely change of scenery.

"All right," Mercy said with a nod. "I think that sounds like a good idea."

Isabella's face relaxed, and her smile brightened. "Oh, good. Good. I'm so glad to hear it. Well, when do you think you might want to make the transition, dear? You can go as soon as you feel up to it."

Seeing no reason to delay the inevitable, Mercy found herself replying, "Now. Let's go now."

CHAPTER 19 OVERWHELM

Mercy

Isabella had insisted on waiting for August to be available in order to take Mercy to the house that they shared in the center of the village. Mercy could understand that. After all, she hadn't exactly proven herself to be the sort of person one could trust not to have a problem on the short walk. For all Isabella knew, she could faint, take off running, or set the house on fire....

Mercy didn't think there was much of a chance of any of those things happening, but that didn't mean Isabella trusted her.

Once August arrived, there was a private conversation in the storage room of the medical center. She heard whispering, but she had no idea what mother and son were talking about. Other than the fact that it was probably about her. She hoped she wasn't stirring up any trouble between the two of them. They were both such wonderful people. She'd hate to come between them in any way.

After a few moments, August walked out first, a smile on his face. "Hi, Mercy," he said. "How are you today?"

"Good," she said, smiling at him. It was easy to smile at someone with such a handsome, kind face. "How are you?"

"Not too bad," he said with an easy smile. "Mom says that you're ready to come home now. Is that right?"

Nodding, Mercy said, "If you think it won't be too much trouble to have me there."

"No, not at all," he said. "I just want to make sure that you understand where you're going and you feel comfortable with it. We have a pretty big house. There are a lot of extra bedrooms because occasionally we host leaders from other packs."

Mercy automatically wondered if the Alpha that had made her start hating that word had ever been in August's house. There was no way for anyone to know that, though, since she still didn't know what had happened to her.

"We decided you should have a room close to my room so that if there's a problem, I can reach you. Mom's room is at the other end of the hallway. Do you think you'd be comfortable in a room near mine? Mom will still be there pretty quickly if you need her."

Mercy nodded, wondering if that's what they'd just been discussing. "I think that's fine."

"Good," August said. "Also, we want you to know that our house is your house. We want you to be completely comfortable there. We have a few Gamma servants who work and live there. They are all very kind people. We'll introduce them to you. Feel free to ask them for anything that you might need."

"All right," Mercy said. It seemed strange that she should have servants, though she didn't know why. Something told her she'd never been in that sort of a situation before, and in fact, there was a good chance that she actually had been the one to do what others asked. But she didn't think she'd been a maid. And she didn't think she'd been treated kindly, the way that it seemed August and Isabella clearly treated the people who worked in their house.

"Do you have any questions?" August asked her.

Mercy shook her head no. She couldn't think of anything she needed to ask.

"All right then. If you're ready to go, then let's go."

Mercy nodded as August stepped over to help her out of the bed.

She knew she could do it alone. She'd been going to the bathroom by herself for several days. But it was nice to have her hand on August's arm, and when she slid her feet to the floor, and he put his other hand on top of hers, she didn't want him to let go.

"All set?" Isabella asked, coming out of the back room. "Let's go home!" She headed to the door and held it open for them.

The sun was bright as Mercy stepped outside for the first time in a while. It hurt her eyes more than she thought it should. She wondered if there was a chance that she wasn't used to being outside.

They walked along down the street. The sounds and scents were a bit overwhelming. Mercy tried to concentrate on the feel of August's arm and let it ground her. Talking, laughing, children playing. A dog barking. The scent of smoke from a fireplace. Meat cooking. Baking bread. All of that incoming information was a bit of a sensory overload.

She wasn't used to it. She could tell. She was used to quiet. She was used to dark and still.

Why?

It didn't take long before August stopped in front of a large white house with lots of windows. "Here we are," he said, pausing to see if she was okay.

Mercy took a deep breath and swallowed hard. As long as no one said those words....

"Welcome to the Alpha's house," August said.

Everything went black.

CHAPTER 20 ROOMIE

August

"Mercy? Mercy? Are you all right?"

It was happening again, and there was nothing August could do to help her or prevent it. All he'd done was welcome her home when he saw her eyes roll back into her head and her body went limp.

He'd caught her, thank goodness. So she wasn't physically injured. But Mercy was lying limp against his arm as he stared into her beautiful face, willing her to open her eyes and look at him.

She did--whether he actually managed to convince her to or she just happened to not have slipped too far away from him this time.

Mercy blinked a few times, a vacant look on her face. At first, he thought maybe she didn't recognize him. The idea of having to start all over again, of trying to explain who he was, where she was, how she'd gotten there one more time, made his heart leap into his throat.

"Are you okay?" he asked her, keeping his voice calm and soft.

"Y-yeah," Mercy said, struggling to stand up. He helped her get back upright. "What happened?" she asked, a hand raised to her head.

"You blacked out a little," he said, still not willing to completely let go of her. "For a few seconds."

"Oh, no," Mercy muttered, shaking her head. "I'm so sorry."

"No! Don't be sorry," August insisted. "Really, you don't need to apologize, Mercy."

She looked around for a few moments, her eyes blinking, potentially not quite focused. "Is this your house?" she asked.

"Yes," August said, determining not to say that A word again that seemed to always send her spiraling. "Would you like to go inside?"

"Sure," Mercy said with a small head bob and a tight smile.

"Perfect." Reluctantly, he let go of her and opened the fence, holding it for her to go through first, and then followed her up the steps.

The door was unlocked, as it almost always was, so he pushed it open and again waited for her to walk in.

Mercy took a few steps into the entryway and paused, sort of in his way. He let her take her time, looking away. "Wow. Your house is really nice," she said, her eyes tracing over the crown molding, down to the banisters of the stairwell, across the wooden floors and flickering back across his mother's carefully chosen furniture and decor.

"Thank you," August said as Mercy took a few more steps inside so that he could come in, too. "Mom did most of it. I just… live here."

She let out a small, polite laugh.

"If you'd like to go upstairs, I'll show you which room will be yours."

Mercy looked confused. She stared at him for a long second before she asked, "Upstairs?"

"Yeah…." August gestured at the staircase in front of them. "The bedrooms are all upstairs. Is that okay?"

"Yes," Mercy said, clearing her throat and shaking her head slightly. "I don't know why, but for some reason… I don't think I was allowed upstairs."

August didn't know what to think about that, so he just said, "Huh. Well, you're certainly allowed upstairs at our house. You can go wherever you'd like."

"Thank you." Mercy's smile was still uncomfortable, and he could tell she didn't like relying on others so completely. He hoped that she'd learn quickly enough that she wasn't a burden on them and that they were glad she was now part of their pack.

Once again, August gestured for her to go up the stairs, and this time, her feet started up the steps. He followed closely behind her, making sure she didn't fall. Blacking out on the stairs could be dangerous.

At the top of the stairs, he took her to the nicest guest room and opened the door. "Here we are. I think you'll like this room. If not, we have others."

Mercy walked in and looked around. He flipped the lights on, which startled her, but then she recovered fairly quickly. "It's lovely. I like the blue bedspread... and the curtains."

"Yeah, there's a pretty good view of Mom's garden out the window." August didn't want to risk doing anything to set her off, so he'd let her look herself, when she was ready. "The bathroom is in there." He lifted his hand toward the half-open door that led to the ensuite.

Mercy was looking at him strangely again. "Bathroom?" she asked.

"Yes. You have your own bathroom."

"Oh." Mercy nodded, but her face was still blank.

"Also... here's the remote," he said, walking over to the dresser where the small black device rested. "I'm not sure if you want to try television again yet... but... here it is." He hoped that the mention of the TV wouldn't upset her.

Mercy looked at the television and nodded. "Great," was all she said.

At least she didn't collapse.

"All right then. If you need anything... uh... I'll be downstairs. Just... give me a holler."

"Okay," she said, still smiling at him.

August didn't want to walk out of the room, but he had no reason to continue to stay except for to stare at her, and that just seemed... creepy.

Giving her a little wave, August stepped out into the hallway and closed the door behind him, letting go a sigh. The idea that he should

go tell his mom that she blacked out again pressed on his mind. But...
Isabella might make her move back to the hospital, and he didn't want
that.

So he'd keep that information to himself--for now.

Hopefully, he wouldn't come to regret that decision....

CHAPTER 21: COVERS

Mercy

THIS WAS THE MOST COMFORTABLE ROOM SHE'D EVER BEEN IN. MERCY was sure of it--even though she couldn't remember a single place she'd been before the healing center. Still, sitting on the end of the bed in the room that August had taken her to, she was certain she'd never been in a room like this before.

Mercy wasn't sure what to do. Part of her wanted to climb into the comfy bed and go to sleep. But she wasn't really tired. It just seemed so inviting. She ran her hand along the soft blue comforter and sighed. What must it be like to live in a house like this? To have so many nice things?

A shower also sounded pleasant. She'd taken a few while she was at the healing center, but she had the feeling that the bathroom attached to this luxurious room had to be unlike any accommodations she'd ever seen in her life.

Mercy kicked off her shoes and took off her socks before letting her bare feet sink into the soft carpet of the floor. A flash of a memory came across her. Cold, concrete. Damp, uncomfortable....

Had she ever stood on carpet so fluffy and warm? Pushing the pictures in her mind aside, she went into the bathroom.

She'd definitely never seen anything like this before. The shower was large enough for three or four people, not that she'd ever want to shower with anyone else. There were plenty of spouts for the water to come out of as well. The bathtub was deep and long enough for her to stretch her legs out straight. She ran her hand along the cool ceramic.

Two sinks behind her with granite countertops, and a toilet in a little room by itself.

Mercy opened the shower door and turned the water on. She looked carefully at the handle to make sure she'd turned it toward the H but not too far. It was something she'd had to learn from Luna Isabella in the healing center. She knew she liked the water warm but not too hot, so she set it accordingly and kept her hand under it until she was certain it was just right.

Stripping out of her clothes was intimidating, even though she knew she was alone. Mercy locked the bathroom door, just in case. She knew she was safe here, that she would have her privacy, but the idea that she had had no privacy before, that she had been looked at when she was in the nude, maybe worse, kept coming back to her. She didn't like the feeling of eyes being on her body.

She stepped beneath the warm water and let it wash away her negative thoughts and work its way over her shoulders. The shower in the healing center had been nice, but this one was amazing. The soaps and shampoos smelled like fragrant flowers. She washed her hair, lathered her body and let the suds soak into her skin and then washed them off.

As she stood beneath the warm water, the drops falling rapidly on her and cascading down her body, another image came to her mind. A man--she couldn't see his face--standing in the distance, in the dark, a bucket of water in his hand as he threw cold water at her. The vision jarred Mercy and she stepped backward, her foot slipping. She caught herself with her hands, bracing against two walls of the shower, but a sizzle of fear pulsated through her, and the glass door of the shower began to vibrate.

"NO!" Mercy shouted, trying to pull back any energy she was about to expel from her body. The last thing she needed to do was shatter the glass shower door in this beautiful bathroom. She took a deep breath and tried to calm herself.

The vibrating stopped, and the door stilled. Mercy placed a hand over her heart, feeling it continuing to hammer in her chest. Whatever it was that had triggered the memory and her reaction was still in her mind. It could get out at any time.

Mercy turned the water off and stepped out, grabbing a fluffy gray towel off of the rack by the door and drying herself off. Fear was still pulsing through her body. She wanted to go hide somewhere so that she couldn't hurt anyone or break anything.

There were clothes hanging in the closet, all of them in her size, with tags on them. They were new. She assumed Luna Isabella had purchased them for her. She got dressed in a comfy pair of pants and a large sweatshirt and then brushed her hair. She was afraid to look in the mirror, though. In her head, she knew that her hair had not been this color for long. Would she see herself in the mirror as she was right now, or would she see a different version of herself?

And would that version trigger another incident?

With her hair still wet, Mercy went into the bedroom and crawled beneath the blankets, pulling them up over her head, blocking out the world.

Unfortunately, the blankets that were covering her memories were slowly being pulled away.

She was beginning to remember.

CHAPTER 22: UNBOXED

A BEAUTIFUL WOMAN HAD JUST MOVED INTO HIS HOUSE.

August was sitting at his desk, doing his best to focus on his work, but his mind kept going back to Mercy. What was she doing right now? Was she okay? Was she sleeping? Was she hungry?

He was trying to focus on the reports he needed to finish looking over, but it was rough with such a huge distraction just down the road. He wanted to go see how she was doing, to see if he could get her anything, but he also knew he had a way of making her feel like her head was going to explode.

August picked up the last report he'd been given and had just started going over it when his phone rang. Part of him was glad for the distraction, but then he looked at the caller ID and saw that it was Rider, the Alpha from Black Hole Moon.

"What do you want, Rider>" August said as he picked up the phone. The last person in the world he wanted to talk to was the Alpha that had been in the picture where Mercy was being abused.

"Oh, come on, August, don't be like that. You know you're glad to hear from me." Even the sound of his voice made August want to scratch the inside of his ears.

"I assure you, that is not the case. What's the matter? Did you lose something again? Maybe your judgment?"

Rider snorted. "If I needed better judgment, I wouldn't be calling you. No, I just had to ask you... has anything gotten destroyed yet?"

Well, the Alpha from Black Hole Moon sure knew how to get his attention.

August had to play it off. He still didn't want to give Rider any indication that Mercy was staying in his pack. "What are you talking about, Rider?"

"August, you and I go way back. I can tell when you're lying, when you're keeping things from me. I know that you have her. Has she broken anything yet? She has quite the temper when she gets... angry."

"Who, Rider? Your mother? Somehow I doubt you are the way that you are because your mother spanked you too much as a child."

"The girl, August. She's there. You have her. My patrols saw your people moving her to your pack not long ago. I know she's there, and I know you are trying to keep her from me because you don't want me to have her power, but I assure you, I have every right to her."

August remembered the last time Rider had called, he'd said he purchased Mercy. "How exactly does one go about buying a person, Rider? I thought the laws about that had changed a long time ago."

"Perhaps for regular shifters, August. But as you know, she is no regular shifter."

"And that makes it okay to buy her? Who even sells people?"

"Why? Are you in the market for your own wench, August?"

"Why would I be if what you're saying is true, Rider? I just want to know what sort of pack Alpha would be so heinous as to sell another human being."

"I'm not telling you that. It doesn't matter," Rider said. "What matters is I want her back. Now."

"Then... I guess you better look somewhere else, Rider. I don't have anything that belongs to you."

"Damn you, August!" Rider shouted. "Is it worth going to war for her? Do you want your packmates to be wounded and killed to protect a girl you don't even know?"

"You can rest assured, if you attack my pack for any reason, Rider, my people will be ready and willing to defend ourselves to the end. I've beaten your ass before, and I can do it again. I strongly suggest you stay on your side of the river. I've already seen footprints that don't belong to any of my patrols on our side of the shoreline. That had better not happen again."

"I can guarantee to you, August, if you do not give her back to me, you will see a whole lot more footprints coming your direction."

"Well, then, Rider, I'll see you in hell."

Rider growled so loudly, August thought he might be in his wolf form for a moment. "I will get Pandora back, August, if it's the last thing I do."

August hung up the phone, shaking with anger. He wanted to run right over to Rider's pack and kick that monster's ass.

He ran his hand through his hair and took a few deep breaths before he realized what Rider had said--Pandora.

Mercy's real name was Pandora.

CHAPTER 23: LID

AUGUST

"HOW DO WE EVEN KNOW THAT RIDER IS TELLING US THE TRUTH?" August's mom asked him from her seat across from his desk. "He could just be messing with us, trying to scare us."

"I'm not scared of her name, Mom. Hell, I'm not even scared of her. Maybe I should be, but I don't think she'd do anything to hurt us."

He could've been putting his entire pack at risk by having a woman he didn't know who clearly had some sort of magical powers in their midst, but it was difficult for him to think that Mercy could be dangerous to him or to anyone else. He was usually a pretty good judge of character, and he felt that Mercy was a good person, that anything that she'd been through in her past wasn't due to her bad character but due to the horrible people she'd been with.

And Rider was a pretty horrible person.

For years, he'd waged war on surrounding packs, attempting to confiscate more territory. He'd killed indiscriminately and even raided some villages where women and children became his victims.

He denied those accusations and said that he'd only ever killed warriors that opposed him, but the battlefield told a different story.

"What do you think will happen if you go over there and tell her what you've discovered, son?" His mother folded her arms in the way she always did when she knew he was making a mistake, and August insisted he was right.

"I don't know. I suppose she'll probably black out again." He picked up a pen and started flipping it over and over in his hand, the tip of it bouncing off of the desk followed by the end, and then the tip again.

"And do you want her to have to go through all of that again? Why not just wait until she's ready? I'm sure she'll remember on her own."

"What if she doesn't remember, Mom? What if the things that happened to her over there were so awful that her mind will not allow her to remember them on her own?"

Isabella cleared her throat. "Well, then, why would you want to be the person to bring that up to her, son?"

August sucked in a deep breath. How was he supposed to argue with that? "I don't know, Mom. I just feel like she needs to remember."

"Her mind is protecting her from her own memories. I think we need to respect that. It would be different if we had no idea where she came from or what had happened to her, and we were trying to find out so that we could take her home. But we know that she's safer here, that she doesn't need to be taken back to where she came from. So let's just give her some time."

"Rider said he bought her, though, Mom. If I can find out where he bought her from, then maybe I can make sure that whoever is out there selling people is punished for doing so."

"There have got to be other ways to do that, August."

She was probably right. She was almost always right. So why was August arguing with her?

He had no idea.

"All right, Mom. I won't tell her. For now. But... I think it's a mistake."

"That's okay, honey. I'll take responsibility for it," Isabella said, standing and reaching across the desk to pat his hand. "I am sure that we need to give her some more time. Let her get accustomed to her surroundings, get more comfortable with all of us, and then... you can gauge how she's doing before you start to dig deeper."

"Fine, Mom." August sighed and dropped his eyes as his mom headed for the door. "Thanks," he called after her, not really wanting to but also trying to be respectful.

She only chuckled, knowing he'd forced it from between his lips.

August continued to flip the pen over and over, listening to the rhythmic tapping. His mind continued to go over what might happen if he were to tell Mercy he knew her real name.

In every scenario he came up with, Mercy blacked out and something was broken.

Perhaps his mom was right and he should keep a lid on this.

If he could.

Sometimes... his mouth did things he didn't want it to.

CHAPTER 24 DRIP

Mercy

It was cold.

Darkness surrounded her, and the smell of dampness filled her lungs. Close to her head, she heard the ping of water falling from above her, landing in a puddle on the concrete, over and over and over again. Dripping, constantly, cutting into her thoughts, eating through her mind. It needed to stop.

But there was no way to make it stop, and as long as she was down here in the damp, dark, cold, she wouldn't be able to do anything to help herself.

How long had she been down here? It seemed like forever. Her stomach felt like it was eating itself, but then, she didn't really have stomach pains anymore because she was so used to being hungry.

She tried to stretch her back, but she couldn't because of the restraints. Why they thought binding her hands around her ankles and tying her ankles together would stop her from using her abilities, she didn't know, but she could still use them.

She could still pick them up and throw them across the room.

She could still blow out the glass in the windows.

She could still burn the entire house to the ground.

It was too bad she couldn't do anything about that damn dripping.

She took a deep breath, lowered her head, and thought about how satisfying it would be to see his head explode, to blow the Alpha's brains right out of his head.

The only problem was, they had something, something important... something precious. And as long as they had that something, she couldn't do anything.

What did they have? It was right there, right in the middle of her mind's eye, right out of focus, right where she couldn't quite reach it.

Drip, drip, drip.

A crack of light cut across her thoughts as she squinted and looked up. "It's time door--"

Mercy sat up straight, not remembering where she was or where she should be. Her heart was hammering in her chest. Her hands shot out around her, feeling her surroundings as she tried to get her breathing under control. Her throat burned as she gasped for air.

She was safe. A look around reminded her that she was at August and Isabella's house. It had all been a dream. But what it was she had been dreaming about, she wasn't sure. As soon as her eyes had opened, much of it had gone away. All she could truly remember was that she was upset, scared, cold.

And that there had been water.

Mercy took a deep breath and ran her hand through her hair, tossing her head back on her pillow and brushing her hair off of her forehead. It was a bit sweaty, baby hairs gripping her skin.

A glance at the clock told her it was the middle of the night--3:14. She could go back to sleep. Her stomach wasn't growling from hunger. She was safe and comfortable. Her heart rate was returning to normal.

Going back to sleep might mean she'd end up right back where she'd been a few moments before. She knew it would be scary to go back there, but if it helped her remember, wouldn't it be worth it?

Or maybe it would be better if she never remembered at all.

Mercy rolled over, pulling her eyes away from the clock. She focused on the wall across from her, telling herself it was all right to let her eyes grow heavy again. It was all right to fade back into sleep, to let the darkness take her. When she opened her eyes again, she'd be right back here, safe and sound in the Alpha's house, her new Alpha, one she could trust. Yes, this is where she really was, where she'd be, no matter where her mind drifted to.

Wasn't it?

CHAPTER 25 BREAKFAST

August

Making breakfast was not something August was particularly good at. Cooking in general was not his forte, but since he couldn't go back to sleep after he woke up at 5:00 in the morning, he decided to get up around 6:00 and go to the kitchen to make breakfast for Mercy.

He'd laid awake for much of the night, thinking about what Rider had told him and the discussion he'd had with his mom. He knew that she was right, that he shouldn't tell Mercy what he'd found out. But at the same time, he hated keeping information from her, too. If he was in her position, wouldn't he want to know what his real name was?

He wanted to say yes to that, but then, he'd never been in a situation where he'd been abused by an entire pack of people, possibly two packs, and then had to run for his life. So maybe if he'd been in a similar circumstance to the one she was fleeing, he wouldn't be so quick to think it would be better if she knew.

He sat down at the island to sip some coffee while the breakfast casserole he'd thrown together was cooking. He'd looked the recipe up online, trying to find the same recipe his grandmother sometimes used, though once he started making this one, he was pretty sure that this one was a little different. It still looked yummy, though. Assuming he didn't screw it up.

While he was sitting there with his phone in his hand, he found himself scrolling through social media pictures, looking for the hashtags that he knew pack members often used. In the half hour it took for the casserole to bake, he didn't find any more pictures of Mercy. Part of him was glad about that, but he was also a little disappointed. He wanted to find as many clues about who she was and where she'd come from as possible.

He'd considered reaching out to Stephanie. She was a lot more reasonable than Rider. It was possible she might give him more information about what was going on with Mercy while she was in Black Hole Moon Pack, but she also might not cooperate with him at all, and she could end up getting information out of him somehow that would be derogatory or harmful to Mercy, so he decided not to do that--not yet anyway.

"Couldn't sleep?"

His mother's voice startled him as he was pulling the casserole out of the oven, and he almost dropped it.

"Uh, no, not really," August said, sitting it on the top of the stove and turning the oven off before he closed the door with his knee.

"I smelled something cooking and was afraid my clock was off, and the servants were already up making breakfast."

"Well, I thought I'd throw something together." August knew she wouldn't believe that he was just cooking for cooking's sake. Isabella raised an eyebrow at him. "All right... for Mercy."

His mom patted his arm. "I'm sure she'll appreciate it. She won't know that you never cook so she should consider herself special, but, I'm sure she'll love it nevertheless."

"Do you want some?" August asked, pulling some plates down from the cabinet.

"Of course. But you try it first."

August turned and looked at her, and she winked at him. "I'm sure it's not poisonous. It might taste as good as when you make it, but it's not going to kill you."

"I didn't say I thought it would, son. I just want to know it doesn't taste awful before I put it in my mouth."

August scooped some out and put it on his plate, pulled a fork out of the drawer and tried it. "It's not bad," he said as the cheesy, egg flavor filled his mouth.

"In that case, sure, I'll have some."

He fixed her a plate and handed it over before going back to his, thinking he'd finish it before he took any up to Mercy, just in case she wasn't awake yet.

As they ate, his mother said, "You know... it seems to me that maybe you're a little smitten with that girl, August. Is that a fair assessment?"

"I don't know if 'smitten' is the right word." He could feel color creeping into his face and tried to fight it.

"Well, honey, I think she's a special girl. Cute, sweet. All of those lovely things. But remember... we don't know anything about her. For all we know, she's married and has children."

August stared at his mother for a moment. He hadn't let the idea of Mercy being married already come to mind. Isabella was right. He needed to slow things down. "I'll keep that in mind, Mom," he assured her.

August fixed a plate for Mercy, put it on a serving tray, got some orange juice and water and put that on the tray as well, and then headed upstairs, reminding himself that he and Mercy were just friends.

CHAPTER 26: NO POKER FACE

Mercy

IT WAS THE DREAMS THAT GOT HER. PULLING HERSELF OUT OF A SOUND sleep filled with awful images, memories coming to life, winding their way around her mind and convincing her that she was there again, in those moments, that's what sucked her down and kept her from moving forward, kept her trapped in a box where she couldn't seem to escape.

Even with her eyes open, staring up at a ceiling lit by the early morning light, wisps of those dreams continued to linger, foggy fingers that crept between her present thoughts and those memories that simply wouldn't come.

She'd been lying awake looking up at the ceiling for about fifteen minutes when there was a light knock on the door. The sky outside told her it was early dawn, the pinks, yellows, and oranges giving her a good idea of the time before she even looked at the clock on the nightstand. She was a little surprised that anyone was knocking this early, but then, she had woken early the last few days when she'd begun to feel better, and she had the idea that she had gotten up early most of her life.

"Yes?" Mercy asked, sitting up and scooting back against the headboard, the blankets pulled up to her chest.

"It's August. I have some breakfast for you. Can I come in?"

Nervous energy danced around in her abdomen. "Of course," Mercy said, excited at the prospect of seeing the Alpha already. She ran her hands through her hair quickly, hoping it wasn't too much of a mess. He'd certainly seen her looking worse.

"Hi," he said with a cheerful smile as he opened the door with one hand, balancing a tray in the other. "I didn't wake you, did I?"

"No, I was awake." She couldn't help but think about how handsome he looked with stubble on his jaw and chin from clearly not having shaved yet.

"Good." He brought the tray over and set it across her lap. "I hope it tastes all right. I'm not much of a cook."

Mercy looked down at the tray on her lap. The plate full of eggs, cheese, and some kind of meat looked really good. "You made this?"

"I did," August said, looking a little sheepish. "I don't cook much, but I woke up a little early this morning, so I decided… what the heck."

Mercy picked up her fork. It was pretty clear he was waiting for her to taste it. She took a bite. "It's really good," she said, chewing with her hand in front of her mouth to cover the food. The taste of cheesy eggs melded together with the flavor of the meat. "You should cook more often."

"Yeah? You're not just being nice are you?"

She laughed. "No, I am not good at lying. You'd be able to tell by my face, I think."

August tipped his head to the side for a second before he asked, "How do you know?"

Raising her eyebrows, Mercy said, "That's a good question. I don't know." It had come out of her mouth as if it were the honest truth, but it wasn't as if she had any memories of trying to tell a fib and being caught.

His smile didn't waver. "Well, I'm glad you're at least starting to sort out who you are," he offered.

Mercy nodded and took another bite of the delicious food he'd brought her. She wondered if it had a name, but she didn't want to ask. She didn't think she'd ever eaten anything like this before.

"What do you think you'd like to do today?" August asked her, still standing next to the bed a little awkwardly.

"Uh... I don't know," Mercy admitted. Her eyes went to the tell vision. It might be fun to watch that again, but not if she might explode it. "What can I do today?"

"Well, if you want, we can go for a walk around the village, and I can show you where everything is. If you think you're up to it. Of course, we don't have to see the whole town in one day, if you get tired."

"No, that sounds great," Mercy said, not sure if she was more excited about seeing the village or spending time with August. "Do you have time for that? Aren't you busy?"

August's smile widened. "I have time."

She wasn't sure if he was good at lying or not, but it definitely looked like he was telling the truth. "Great."

"All right. I'll let you eat and get ready. Do you want to just come downstairs when you're ready?"

"Sure," Mercy said, wanting to scarf down the rest of the food so she could run off with him.

"Cool. If you need help getting down the stairs, just shout, and we'll come help."

"All right." Mercy thought it would be a little embarrassing to have to do that. She thought she could make it anyway.

August left, and Mercy took a deep breath, trying to get her heart to settle down in her chest.

She shouldn't be so excited to be going out to walk around town with a man she just met--but she was.

And she didn't think anything was going to change that.

CHAPTER 27 THE VILLAGE

Mercy

The village was a lot different than Mercy had envisioned it, though she had no idea why. Walking down the main street next to August, she was surprised at all of the people, all of the bustle, all of the flurry. It started to feel a little overwhelming from time to time, so she had to remind herself to focus on the Alpha beside her and not on the noise and potential chaos all around her.

She'd chosen a comfortable pair of jeans, a white long sleeved shirt, and a brown jacket, along with some brown boots that fit perfectly and a bright scarf. She loved how the colors in the scarf matched the leaves falling from the trees. She had a feeling she didn't usually have clothes like this. When she'd been found, she'd been wearing a tattered dress; it was her impression that she often wore the same dress, day after day, without a shower or a bath.

"This is the coffeehouse," August said, pointing to a place that smelled wonderful. "And over there is the pizza parlor. We don't have a lot of restaurants, just the pizza place and the diner down the street." He pointed ahead of them, and Mercy's eyes went along the paved road toward the other buildings up ahead, but she didn't know which one he was talking about yet.

He showed her the post office, the general store, a couple of boutiques, and then they got to the diner. It smelled really good, too, though she wasn't hungry. She'd eaten all of the breakfast August had brought her. She was also under the impression that eating wasn't something she had done regularly, and when she had eaten, it wasn't much.

"Do you want to have a seat on that bench over there and rest for a while?" August asked, gesturing to a bench beneath a tree full of leaves the same shades as her scarf.

"Sure," Mercy said, walking alongside him as he headed that way. He looked as handsome as ever in jeans and a blue button-down shirt that made his eyes especially bright. He smelled a lot like the forest, a hint of pine and maybe leather. Smelling him was almost as pleasant as standing outside of the coffeehouse or the diner. She hadn't smelled anything from the pizza parlor, but she got the impression that pizza wasn't a breakfast food.

They sat with a few inches of space between them. Several people came by and said hello to them, showing the sign of respect to August with their fist touching their shoulder and their heads bowed. He always humble acknowledged them. Mercy wondered how he ever got anything done when he was constantly having to say hello to everyone that was walking past them.

"Do you think you might be interested in having a job at one of these places someday?" August asked. "Not that you have to, but you could. If you wanted to."

Mercy stared at him for a long moment, not sure what to think about that. Eventually, she said, "I think I would like to have a job and contribute, but I'm not sure what I would be good at. I don't know what skills I have."

"Most of these jobs aren't too hard. The boutique is just hanging and folding clothes, helping people pick out gifts, and working the cash register. You can probably learn to work in the bakery or the diner easily enough. But like I said, you don't have to work if you don't want to."

"If I don't work, what will I do?" Mercy asked, imagining that all of the pack members had to contribute in one way or another.

"Uh... well... a lot of the Omegas patrol the border and train, in case we are attacked. The Gammas do other jobs...."

"Like cleaning and that sort of thing, right?"

"That's right." August gave her an odd look, and Mercy just shrugged. She wasn't sure how she knew that either. "We don't really know what you did in your last pack, so I suppose if you didn't want to do any of those jobs, we could just... find you something else to do here."

Mercy was quiet for a moment, thinking about what she might've done in her old pack. She thought she might have been a Gamma. But she didn't think she cleaned or served anyone, not in the regular sense of the word. Not like the Gammas that worked in August's house that she'd seen in the hallways and knew they were the ones who cleaned and usually the ones who made the food--when the Alpha didn't want to.

"But like I said, if you don't want to work, you don't have to," August continued.

"So I'll just... live in your house forever and do nothing to contribute?" Mercy asked, arching an eyebrow at him.

"No, I mean. You'll contribute, I bet. Whether you work or not. But you can stay in our house as long as you want to."

"And what about when there's a Luna--other than your mother?" Mercy continued. "Do you think your wife will mind the strange girl who lives in your house and does nothing?"

August's face turned almost as red as the leaves above him as he tried to find a reasonable response. Mercy sort of liked knowing that she could make him turn different colors. She smiled at him and then looked away. "I will try to remember what I used to do. I think I was very good at it. But... I think... it might've been... dangerous."

CHAPTER 28: DANGER ZONE

"Dangerous?"

August couldn't help but repeat the last word Mercy had said. The look on her face at the moment was more of a vacant stare than anything threatening, but the fact that she thought her old job was something other than a regular role any woman might play in a pack would've set anyone on edge.

He wasn't shocked, though. He'd seen the pictures. Likewise, he'd seen what she could do.

"I'm not sure why I think that." Mercy's eyes began to focus again, and she turned to look at him, a hint of a smile on her face, her cheeks pinking just slightly, as if she were embarrassed by what she'd just said. "It's just… something that comes to mind. Maybe it's because of what happened with the tell vision."

"Television." He corrected her with an encouraging smile so that she would know he wasn't making fun of her, just trying to help. "Do you think that you were dangerous to other people, though, Mercy? Or is it possible it was you that was in danger?"

Her forehead crinkled. "I don't know," she admitted. "I mean... I was running from something. Is it possible that I only think I was dangerous because of the way I was treated?"

He couldn't help but reach over and put his hand on top of hers where it rested between them on the bench. "I can't imagine you purposely hurting anyone, Mercy. Not unless you had to in order to protect yourself or someone that you loved."

"Someone I loved...." Mercy repeated his words, and that look came about her again, like she was trying to pull a memory out of the far reaches of her mind, and it just wouldn't resurface. "Do you think there might be people in my other pack that I loved?" she asked. "Is it possible that there are people there who are upset that I am gone?"

"I don't know," August admitted. "That is, I don't know if there are people who love you and care about you that are upset that you're gone. I can imagine there must be somewhere, but I don't know if they're at Bl--" He stopped himself. He didn't want to say the words again. The last thing he needed was to cause an episode right here in the open amidst his pack members. He thought maybe he should get Mercy home. They probably shouldn't be talking about these potentially explosive topics in public.

"Black Hole Moon?" Mercy asked, after August had stopped short of saying the name of the pack he knew she'd run from.

August nodded, not sure how she was tolerating the name now when she'd been anything but calm the last time she'd heard those words said in succession.

"Do you think I may have been in a different pack before that?" Mercy asked him.

"I think it's possible," he said with a nod.

"Why do you think that?"

He couldn't answer that without telling her everything that he'd learned from talking to Rider. Telling her he'd talked to that particular person couldn't be good for her. So... he decided to put that discussion off. "I don't know. I just think it might be that you weren't there forever. Maybe you would've run before now if you'd been there your whole life."

"Or maybe I couldn't escape from the other place either." She shook her head slowly, not looking at him. "I wish I could remember."

"Maybe it's best if you don't remember, at least for a while," he said. "Until you're ready to remember."

"You might be right." Mercy said. "Do you want to go back to your house now?"

"I think that might be a good idea. You should probably rest."

Mercy nodded, and August stood, offering her his hand so that she could get up off of the bench. When they turned around to walk home, she didn't let go.

CHAPTER 29 THE EXPLORER

Mercy

Television was quickly becoming one of Mercy's favorite things. August had shown her how to use the remote control for the contraption in the living room, explaining that the one in her room was the same, and told her she could watch while he went and worked on a few things in the office. He'd also told her she could help herself to anything in the kitchen or ask one of the servants to make her something.

Mercy didn't know how she felt about asking anyone else to cook for her, so when she'd gotten hungry, she'd wandered into the kitchen to have a look around. Now, she was sitting on the couch with a can of something called Diet Pepsi on the table next to her, along with a bag of Doritos, marshmallows, and something called Chex Mix. She wasn't sure if any of these things were meant to be eaten the way that she was eating them, just one piece at a time, or if they were ingredients that were meant to make something else, but she was enjoying them. She had learned that the Doritos and Chex Mix taste fine together, but the marshmallows did not taste okay with anything else, including the Diet Pepsi, which she also wasn't sure she was a fan of.

She liked the bubbles, but after she swallowed, her mouth tasted a little funny.

On the television, she was watching a group of people sitting on an orange couch talking about things that happened in their lives while they drank a whole bunch of coffee. She wondered if coffee would taste better with Doritos than Diet Pepsi but she didn't know if she could figure out how to make any. She thought she'd smelled it earlier when they'd passed the coffeehouse earlier. It was the same scent she smelled coming from Isabella's cup sometimes. It didn't smell like it would taste good with Doritos.

Most of what the people on the television were talking about was foreign to her, so she didn't laugh much when the ghost people laughed. She didn't think they were actually ghosts, but every time one of the people on the orange couch said something, there was laughter from somewhere other than the other people sitting around, so she didn't know if this coffeehouse was haunted or if maybe the friends were being spied on, but she kept watching to find out.

Every once in a while, someone else would come on the screen and tell her about something amazing--like shoes that would make her run faster or cheeseburgers that could be made however she wanted. Again, she couldn't sort out what this had to do with the orange couch people, but she figured if she watched long enough, she could sort it out.

"Hi, Mercy!"

Isabella's voice had her head turning away from the television. "Hi," she said. "How are you?"

"Good. I just came home for lunch. Then I've got to go back to the healing center. Are you...." Isabella made a strange face as she looked at the items Mercy had on the couch with her, but then she smiled. "Do you want a sandwich? Or a salad maybe?"

"Oh, uh... okay," she said. "I just have to figure out what this man with the crunchy looking hair is going to do about his teeth being too white."

Isabella stepped into the living room and looked at the television.

"You're watching *Friends*, I see. I never got into it, but it's supposed to be a very funny show."

"The ghost people seem to think so," Mercy said.

Again, Isabella was looking at her oddly. "Ghost people?"

"Yeah, the people that keep laughing. I can't see any of them so--"

Isabella covered her mouth with her hand for a second, but when she pulled it away, she had a hint of a smile that made Mercy think maybe she'd been about to laugh. "That's the studio audience, dear. Or a laugh track. Some shows are shot in front of a group of live people, and others just make it sound like that. They figure if you hear people laughing, you'll laugh, too."

"Oh." She tipped her head to the side and tried to make sure she'd understood everything Isabella had said. A studio audience? Shot? Laugh track? She didn't really know any of those words, but she got the idea that the laughing wasn't really part of the show.

"I can fix you a sandwich while you watch. Do you want tuna fish? Or maybe ham and cheese?"

Mercy had had ham and cheese before when she was at the healing center, but she wasn't sure about tuna. It might be nice to try something new. "Whatever you're having is fine," she said.

A few minutes later, Isabella brought her a plate with a sandwich on it that smelled kind of funny. For some reason, Mercy thought it smelled like the river, but she didn't know why.

Isabella sat down on the other side of the couch, putting some of the Doritos on her plate. Maybe she'd been right and Doritos were supposed to be eaten the way she was eating them--though not with the marshmallows.

Mercy took a bite of her sandwich. It tasted weird, and she wasn't sure she liked it, but she wasn't going to complain. She decided to just eat it and wash it down with her Diet Pepsi. Isabella laughed a little at the friends on the television, and Mercy laughed, too, because she realized she was supposed to.

After they finished their sandwiches, Isabella took the plates back into the kitchen and Mercy decided to change the channel to see if something better was on. She really had no idea what kind of shows she might like. Flipping through the channels the way that August had shown her, she saw all kinds of things. Some were in black and white, which was strange. Others were drawings. She tried to watch each one for a few moments to see if it was interesting before changing the channel.

She stopped on a channel where there was a drawing of a little girl talking to a monkey. It looked like it was probably for little kids, so she was about to change the channel again when one of the characters said something to the little girl that had Mercy frozen stiff.

"Let's go find the treasure, Dora!" he said.

The remote fell from her hand as she tried to understand why her heart was pounding in her chest. A song started playing and they just kept saying the little girl's name over and over and over again.

Mercy closed her eyes, trying to shut it out. She didn't want to explode the television. Not again. A spray of something wet hit her in the face and she realized she'd exploded the Diet Pepsi can instead. It popped so loud, Mercy jumped and screamed.

Isabella came running back into the room. "Mercy! What's the matter?"

When Mercy opened her mouth again, she couldn't control what was coming out of it. All she could do was repeat the same word over and over again, just like the song.

"Dora, Dora, Dora, Dora, Dora, Dora!"

CHAPTER 30: RUSH

August ran out of his office so quickly and without an explanation, he was certain Beaux probably thought he was crazy, but the moment his mother's voice filled his head that he needed to come home, that something was wrong with Mercy, he'd got up and exited as fast as possible, leaving his Beta standing there, calling his name.

"Sorry--it's Mercy," he said, using the mind-link, as he was almost home. "Catch me up later." They'd been talking about the new patrol schedule Beaux wanted to put in place to make sure the Omegas were well rested and every patrol had a fair amount of warriors on it. August thought it was a great idea, but he wasn't about to sit and listen to another word when something was wrong with Mercy.

His mom hadn't said what it was, and she wasn't responding to his mind-link messages. So... he'd have to find out for himself.

He ran through the front door and found Mercy lying on the couch with blood dripping from her ears--both of them this time. His mother had a tissue pressed to each of them. Mercy's eyes were closed, but every half a second or so, her body twitched.

"What happened?" he asked, seeing a mess of chips and marshmallows on the floor and Diet Pepsi can that looked like it'd been squeezed by a vise.

"I don't know!" Isabella said. "One minute, she was fine. We had lunch. She was watching TV. I'd gone into the kitchen. When I came back... I found her sitting here screaming the same thing over and over again."

"What was she saying?" August asked, lowering himself to his knees next to his mom so that he was closer to Mercy's head.

"Uh... I couldn't really understand it," Isabella said with a shrug. "It sounded like 'door.' I thought maybe someone had come to the door and it scared her, but there was no one there."

"What was on the television?" August asked brushing Mercy's hair back off of her forehead.

"Some cartoon," Isabella said. "I turned it off, and that's when she stopped screaming and fell over."

August turned and picked up the remote control off of the floor. He didn't want Mercy to see or hear anything that would upset her again, so he turned the speakers off before he turned the TV back on.

It was a cartoon, that was true. But as soon as he saw what it was, he understood what had to have happened. August didn't watch a lot of cartoons, but he knew what this one was called because he'd seen plenty of little girls in the pack wearing shirts with her picture or carrying dolls that looked the same as the girl on the screen. He turned the TV back off.

"What was it?" Isabella asked.

"Dora the Explorer," he replied.

Isabella's eyebrows knit together. "Why in the world would that--"

He got close to her ear and whispered, "Pandora."

"Oh." Isabella sank down further on her knees. "I didn't even consider--"

"I know." August shook his head. "It's just a good thing you were here when it happened. If she'd been alone... who knows what might've happened."

"I guess we can't leave her alone anymore."

"Let's see how she is when she wakes up before we decide anything. This might've helped the situation." August was trying to be optimistic.

"She's bleeding from both ears, Augie. I don't think it could possibly be a good thing." Isabella pulled the tissues away. The bleeding had stopped, but he understood why his mom was still so concerned. He even pardoned the childhood nickname that usually made him cringe.

Since there wasn't anything to say in response to that, August just waited, brushing Mercy's hair back, hoping that she woke up soon. If she was going to be back in a coma for even a little while, he wasn't sure he was going to be able to handle that.

It didn't take long for them to find out.

Mercy began to stir only a few minutes after August arrived, and then, after opening her eyes and blinking for a moment, she tried to sit up.

"Be careful, honey," Isabella said. "Take your time."

Mercy pressed a hand to her head and leaned back against the couch. "Wh-what happened?"

"You passed out again," August said, taking his hands off of her but staying ready to catch her if need be.

Mercy stared blankly for a few moments and then looked at August and said, "I know my name."

CHAPTER 31: THE DARKNESS

Mercy

AUGUST WAS LOOKING AT HER LIKE HE WASN'T SURE WHAT TO THINK OF her when Mercy announced that she knew her name. "You do?" he asked, as if he wasn't sure if it was a good thing or a bad thing.

She nodded, not sure whether she should continue to think of herself as Mercy or use the name she was certain she'd been given at birth--by someone. She still couldn't remember if she had parents or not, but she was certain of her name.

August cleared his throat. 'Uh... what is it?"

"Mari," she said quietly. "My name is Mari."

August's eyebrows knit together, and he exchanged a confused glance with his mother. "Mari?" he repeated. "Are you certain of that?"

She nodded. She wasn't sure of anything else, but she knew that her name was Mari.

"If that's the case, dear," Isabella said, "why did that cartoon make you so upset?"

She shook her head slowly back and forth. "I'm not exactly sure. The girl's name in the cartoon--Dora--it reminded me of some terrible things that happened to me, but I don't know exactly what they were. I just know there was pain. I remember a dark place, and some sort of chains. I don't know what else happened to me, but when I heard her name, it reminded me of what they shouted."

August slid closer to her, grasping her hand. "What who shouted at you, Mercy? Uh, Mari?"

"I don't know." In her mind, a fight was going on between her will to remember and whatever part of her brain was fighting to preserve itself from the dangers of remembering. "I just remember they were evil, awful people. And they put me someplace scary and hurt me."

"Mari--" August began, but she cut him off.

"You can call me Mercy if you want to. I like it better."

"Are you sure?" he asked. She nodded. "Okay. Mari, I've spoken to someone who claims to have known where you came from, and he says that you have a different name, that it's not Mari."

"You've spoken to someone who knows where I came from?" She could hardly believe what he was telling her. "When? How long have you known?"

"Not long," he said, though there was something in his eyes that made her think that wasn't exactly true. "I didn't want to tell you because I didn't want to upset you."

That was understandable. She tucked her hair behind her ear. "Who was it?"

Again, August and Isabella exchanged glances, and then his mother shrugged. "His name is... Rider."

"Rider?" Mercy repeated the name, not just because she wanted to make sure she heard him correctly but also because she wanted to see how that name fit on her tongue. She reached into her mind for a memory, any memory, of someone by that name. But she came up empty. "Who is he?"

"He's from another pack... a nearby pack. One on the other side of the river."

"The river I came through to get into your pack lands?"

August nodded. "He says that he bought you, and that your name is... Pandora."

Mercy took a deep breath in, remembering that that was what they'd been shouting at her--not Dora but Pandora. Her head began to ache, and she had to lean forward with her head in her hands to keep from getting queasy.

The couch shifted as August wrapped his arm around her. "You're safe now," he reminded her. "It doesn't matter what happened before, Mercy. You're here now, and we're going to keep you safe."

The pain in her head was almost blinding, and she was afraid she was going to pass out again. She found herself grappling to gain some sort of grasp on August. His arms were strong around her, but she still felt like she was sliding away from him. "C-can you take m-me upstairs?" she managed.

"Of course," he said.

He picked her up as if she only weighed a pound or two and carried her toward the stairs. Mercy buried her head in his chest, trying to fight the pain in her head, but it was winning, and she was beginning to feel herself slipping under again. It was like a current of water, dragging her down so deep that no light could penetrate there.

No, it wasn't like that. It was like... she was being shoved inside of a box, and someone was closing the lid, cutting off all of the light, all of the sound... all of the air.

CHAPTER 32: NOT A DREAM

MARI?

August was so confused. Why in the world had Rider called her Pandora if her name was Mari? And why did that stupid cartoon make her so upset if Dora wasn't her name?

Like everything else when it came to Mercy, there didn't seem to be any easy answers, just more mysteries. She was lying on his shoulder, asleep, and he sort of felt like he should pull his arm from beneath her and let her sleep alone, but at the same time, she'd seemed to want him to stay.

Or maybe he just wanted him to stay.

None of this was adding up, and he really felt like it was time to get some answers. Perhaps he should go over to Black Hole Moon and see what Rider would tell him. Maybe there was someone in that pack who could tell him what he needed to know. A lot of Black Hole Moon members were shady. Perhaps he could bribe one or two of them.

Or he could just go get Rider, bring him back here, tie him to a chair, and get the information out of him.

August was still imagining how much fun it would be to beat the shit out of Rider when he realized Mercy was stirring in his arms.

It wasn't a gentle tossing either. It was tumultuous, like a stormy sea. "Mercy?" August said, not sure if he should shake her more or try to still her. "Mercy? You're okay. It's a dream. It's just a dream."

Her eyes flew open, wide. Even though the room was a little dark, he could see the whites of her eyes, and they looked like they were glowing just a tad.

She didn't seem to know where she was or who he was. "Mercy? It's me. August. You're okay. You're safe. Were you dreaming?"

She nodded and then looked around before she finally let out the breath she'd been holding since her eyes opened.

"You're all right," he assured her. "No one can hurt you here."

She settled down onto the pillow, and August started to pull his arm out, trying not to be so intrusive, but she refused to let him pull it free. Her hand clenched around his arm, keeping him still.

"Do you remember what you were dreaming about?" he asked, keeping his voice soft.

She nodded again. "Yes. It was… a box. A dark box. And I was inside. I couldn't get out, and I could hardly breathe." Tears slipped out of her eyes and down her cheeks as she recounted the horrifying dream.

"It was just a dream," he reminded her, brushing the tears from her cheeks.

"No, it wasn't, August. It wasn't just a dream."

She looked so beautiful lying there in his arms, her eyes so wide and shimmery in the dim light. Her frailness, her petite body curled against him, made him want to do whatever he could to protect her. "You're fine now, Mercy. You're here with me. That was a nightmare."

"But it wasn't just a dream," she insisted, tugging on his shirt sleeve.

August took a deep breath and brushed her hair off of her face, wishing there was something he could do or say to make her understand that he wouldn't let anything happen to her. "Mercy--you're not in a box. You're in my home, your home for as long as you want it to be. Trust me when I say nothing bad can happen to you here."

"I believe you, August," she said, her grip relaxing slightly. "That still doesn't negate the fact that it wasn't a dream."

"Mercy--"

She cut him off. "It was a memory."

CHAPTER 33: BRUSH

Mercy

"A MEMORY?" AUGUST REPEATED.

Mercy nodded. She could tell by his expression he wasn't sure what to think about her confession. While she wasn't sure how she knew that the images she had of being placed inside a dark box were a memory and not a dream, she was certain that that was the case.

August cleared his throat. She watched his Adam's apple bob up and down. It was late in the afternoon now, and he had stubble along his square jaw and down his throat. The urge to reach up and touch him, to run her thumb along his chin, to feel that stubble bite into her flesh, was overwhelming. How would he react? What if, instead of dragging her thumb along his flesh, it was her lips. Would he recoil in horror, or would he welcome it?

As he began to speak, Memory tried to focus her thoughts on his words and not the visions in her mind. "Mercy, did you remember anything else?"

She shook her head. "No, not yet. Just that it was dark, damp, and musty. I couldn't see anything--not after the lid was closed. It was pitch black. Even though my eyesight is pretty good. That's because we're shifters, right?" she asked, waiting for him to nod. "I still couldn't even see my hand in front of my face."

"Do you remember any sounds?"

Mercy tipped her head to the side and tried to remember. It took her a moment. Faintly, the idea that there was a banging in the back of her mind. It wasn't rhythmic; it was sporadic. Sometimes louder, sometimes softer. She nodded. "Some sort of a banging sound."

Now it was August's turn to crank his head sideways. "What kind of banging? Like a hammer?"

"I don't think so," she said. "I don't know." She wished she could tell him more, but nothing else was coming to mind.

"Did you smell anything?"

"Just… damp. You know, a musty smell?"

"Like concrete?"

She nodded. "Maybe… wet wood?" Did she even know what that smelled like?

Yes--she did. She'd smelled it in the woods, right before she'd collapsed. Before August's Omegas had found her.

He lifted a hand and smoothed her hair back. "Whatever it was that you remembered, Mercy. Wherever it was… it's just a dream. And it's over now. You don't have to worry about ever being there again, okay?"

She nodded. While the thought of where she'd been before was still terrifying, with his arms around her, she felt safer than she had since she arrived. She felt safer than she ever had in her life. She knew that to be the case, even if she couldn't even say where she'd been before she'd arrived here.

She knew he needed to go, that he was the pack Alpha and had work to do, but the idea of him getting up, of him walking out of the room and leaving her all alone with her dreams, made her nervous.

"Are you all right?" he asked, as if he could feel her shaking.

Mercy took a deep breath. "I just… I don't think I want to be alone. I mean, I think… I've been alone a lot. And it's scary."

"Don't worry, Mercy. I won't go anywhere."

"But you're the Alpha. Don't you have things to do?"

He smiled at her and brushed his fingers along her cheek. "I have an excellent Beta."

Mercy smiled, too, wishing it was true that he could just hold her forever.

Maybe he couldn't hold her forever, but he could hold her for now. She buried her head in his chest and rested her hand on his other shoulder. As Mercy began to fall back to sleep, she felt the soft brush of August's lips on the top of her head.

Maybe falling asleep wasn't so bad after all.

CHAPTER 34: PROBLEMS

AUGUST

AUGUST HAD A PROBLEM.

As the pack Alpha, he was used to having problems. In fact, he usually liked having problems. His ability to reason through a tricky situation and come up with a solution was always something he enjoyed, particularly when he came up with creative solutions that other people may have never considered. Having problems to solve gave him meaning; it gave him purpose.

Yet, this problem was not one he was enjoying whatsoever. August needed to figure out a way to deal with this problem without making the entire situation worse.

Sitting behind his desk, he tapped a pen against the edge, letting the dull thump of plastic on wood take his mind away from the thoughts that had begun churning days ago and were finally beginning to catch up with him, but the distraction only lasted a few seconds.

He couldn't stop thinking about Mercy.

And it wasn't just her predicament that was weighing on his mind, it was the girl herself.

Last night, she'd fallen asleep in his arms, and he hadn't been able to leave her. Not until the sun was coming up. He'd finally managed to lay her down and sneak out a couple of hours before he needed to be at work, but for hours he'd just laid there with her head resting on his chest, breathing in her sweet scent, and feeling the soft, satiny skin of her arm beneath his hand. The weight of her on top of him was as comforting as a favorite blanket in the wintertime, and he never wanted to let her go.

And that was a problem.

Because not only did he really and truly not know anything about her, she didn't know anything about herself.

For all they knew, she was married.

He didn't think that was the case, but he had no way of knowing for sure, and neither did she.

Sighing, August ran his hand through his hair and looked at his work. He needed to do something to take his mind off of her, but there didn't seem to be anything at all that he could do. Every time he started to work on a new project, his mind quickly wandered back to Mercy.

Finally, after several hours of trying, August got up and went outside.

He should've been exhausted after not getting any sleep the night before, but he could feel the adrenaline pulsing through his veins. He barely made it to the edge of the woods before he felt himself starting to shift.

August stripped out of his clothing quickly so that he didn't tear it and then let his wolf run wild. It hadn't been that long since he went for a run, but it felt like he hadn't been in the woods in forever. He shot over the ground, between trees, leaping over boulders, flying through puddles, letting his wild side completely take over.

He had no idea how long he was out there running, but it seemed like a long time before he finally circled back for home. He'd stayed in his own territory; he knew that much. But after running for so long at full speed, his legs were beginning to ache a bit as he made the loop back around to go home. It was a good ache, one that reminded him that he was alive.

August found himself near the river as he headed back toward his village. He slowed along the banks, his eyes wandering across to the other side. He had the distinct feeling that someone was watching him, though he didn't know who or where they were.

He should've been concerned, a lone wolf out by himself far from his village with potential enemies within striking distance.

But he wasn't frightened at all. He didn't have the feeling that whoever was watching him was dangerous--just observing.

His eyes traced through the trees across the creek. He took his time, really looking closely.

Then, he saw her.

The moment his eyes landed on the small form of a wolf in the distance, she turned and ran off, heading back toward the village in Black Hole Moon. But August had seen her just the same.

He assumed it was a female wolf due to the size and the feminine look of her eyes and shape of her face. He hadn't gotten a great look at her, but his eyes had searched her out. Her fur was dark and shaggy, which made her stand out against the green of the pine trees that she was standing behind.

Part of him wanted to follow her, to track her down and ask her who she was and what she wanted, but August couldn't do that. He'd be crossing into another pack's land. Besides, there was no reason to frighten her.

Maybe if he was nice, she'd come back. And if she came back, maybe she'd come closer. And if she came closer... maybe he could find out what she knew about Mercy.

He didn't know much about that other wolf, but he had a pretty good idea that she did, in fact, know Mercy.

And that meant August needed to know her.

CHAPTER 35: NOT POSSIBLE

Mercy

WATCHING TELEVISION HAD NOT QUITE WORKED OUT FOR MERCY either time that she had tried it, so she decided to spend her day reading a book. Luna Isabella had recommended something called *Little Women* to her, which she said was a classic, and so far, Mercy was enjoying it.

She'd curled up in the window seat in the bedroom she'd been sleeping in. Outside, fall leaves fluttered from the trees, spreading a blanket of color all over the velvety lawn. Mercy's eyes kept wandering away from the words, even though she did like the book. Once her eyes strayed from the words, they quickly slipped to August.

She'd basically forced him to sleep with her the night before. Well, not sleep with her sleep with her. Even her amnesia didn't wipe out the understanding of what that meant. But she had trapped him in her bed by falling asleep on his chest. When she'd awoken and he was gone, it had been painful but understandable. He had work to do.

Mercy wondered if she had work to do, too. Did she have duties at her last pack? Had she been something important? A healer? A warrior? She didn't think so. Her memories seemed to establish that she had been hidden away wherever she was before, though she didn't know why or by whom.

She thought that it probably had something to do with her magical powers. Could it be that the people in the last pack were afraid of her?

Did they have a reason to be afraid of her?

Could she harm people with these powers that she had? Could she control them better than she had been?

The urge to attempt to do something with her powers was over-whelming, but Mercy was afraid, especially since she was in August and Isabella's home. She didn't want to break or ruin anything else.

He would help her. She knew that he would. If she asked him to, he'd help her with anything. She wasn't quite sure how she knew that, but it was one thing she knew for certain.

Why he would help her, she also didn't know. It was too much to hope that he was feeling the same way about her as she w

as about him. After all, he knew nothing about her, and she couldn't fill him in. How could he be falling for someone who had no past? Or had a past that no one would ever know anything about?

On the other hand, she knew plenty about August. She hadn't been in the pack very long, but she'd already established who he was. He was the Alpha, a strong leader, someone who was devoted to his pack members above anything else. He was someone who loved to help other people and wouldn't fail to do anything he could to help others.

He was kind and smart and loving and... handsome.

Goddess, was he handsome. Did people use that word? He was hot. He was sexy. He made her body tingle with the briefest touch, and when she'd been lying in his arms, not only had she felt safe, she'd felt urged.

Urged to kiss him. Urged to touch him. Urged to ask him to touch her.

Was that wrong?

She didn't know, but she couldn't control it.

She'd have to learn to, though because it was too much to ask of him. He'd already given her so much and gone out of his way to do so many things for her, asking him to give more of himself would be so completely selfish of her.

Unless he felt the same way about her already….

Mercy sighed and pulled her eyes away from the window and back to her book. She'd just have to figure out how to stop thinking of August as anything more than a friend.

If that was even possible.

CHAPTER 36: COFFEE CONFIDENTIAL

"Where did you see her?"

August spun his coffee cup back and forth slightly as he attempted to answer his mother's questions. He'd been back from his run for a few hours. Working in the office after seeing the dark wolf watching him from the shoreline had not worked out well. So, he'd come home, thinking it would do him some good to speak to his mother.

So far, he didn't feel any better about it, though. Isabella was only asking him questions he didn't want to answer.

"She was out by the river, near the place where Mercy was found."

"And she was just standing there? Behind the trees?"

He nodded. They'd been over this.

"How do you know it was a female?" His mother was also drinking coffee, but her hands weren't shaking like his were, so she was holding her cup up in front of her mouth taking frequent sips.

"I guess I don't know for sure." August ran a hand through his hair and took a deep breath. Why was he so bothered by this? He needed to focus on the positive. There was another wolf out there, one he could potentially speak to. One that might know Mercy's story. That could help him to keep her safe. "The wolf was small, and the face looked feminine to me."

"But it was hard for you to see through the trees, right?"

"Yes. That's why I'm not sure."

Isabella took another drink of her coffee before she sighed and blew out a loud exhale "Well, I suppose all you can do is alert the patrols. See if they can get her to come with them to speak to them."

"I don't think she will want to come across the river if there's a chance she could get caught."

"She'd have to know we wouldn't hurt her if she's trying to help Mercy, wouldn't she?"

"I don't think it would be us she'd be afraid of," August clarified. "If her own pack members found out she was over here speaking to us, she could end up in trouble with them. And from what Mercy's told me, getting in trouble in Black Hole Moon is traumatizing."

Isabella tapped her fingernails on the table the way she did when she was thinking. "There's a chance that Mercy wasn't mistreated while she was in Black Hole Moon."

"I have a picture of it, Mom."

"All right. That's true. But I'm just saying, these images she's seeing, the ones where she feels that she's being locked in a box--they might've taken place somewhere else. We know she was in another pack before she came there."

"We don't know that for sure. That's just what Rider said, and I tend not to believe a damn word he says." August tried to take a drink of his coffee, but the liquid was cold and too bitter, so he spit it back in the cup before he moved it away from his mouth and then slid the mug away.

"What do you think you want to do, son?" Isabella was looking at him in a way that told him regardless of what his answer was, she wouldn't approve.

"I think I need to go find her," he said. "Or go wait for her to come back."

"What if she doesn't come back? Will you cross into their territory to find her?"

"I don't want to," he admitted. It wasn't that he was afraid of Black Hole Moon's warriors. He just didn't want to give Rider and his pack any reason whatsoever to come onto his territory, and if a rival Alpha was found on another pack's lands, that was all the reason he would need to invite himself over. Not that his people hadn't been crossing over into August's territory. He had reason to go over there as well, but so far, he was trying to avoid it. There was no reason to get his people hurt if he could avoid it.

"Whatever you decide to do, be careful, honey. I know how much you care about her, but I don't want to see you getting hurt. It's not worth it to help her remember something she doesn't want to remember."

August nodded. He understood what his mother was saying. Perhaps it wasn't that he wanted Mercy to remember where she came from.

Maybe he just wanted to know for himself.

CHAPTER 37: OUT

Mercy

Mercy lay awake in her bed, on her back, staring up at the ceiling. She'd been lying there for hours, thinking about the possibility of falling asleep, and what it would mean once she started to dream.

Lately, the only time she slept well was when she was asleep on August's chest. That hadn't been frequent enough. While he had offered to help her any way that he could, it seemed a bit silly for her to ask him to spend the night in her room with her every night. After all, she was a grown woman. And she should be able to fall asleep and have tranquil dreams without having someone with her.

Yet, here she was, in the middle of the night, watching the shadows from the trees outside of her window trace across the ceiling, wondering when she would fall asleep, and if she fell asleep, what horrible dreams she might have.

Would it be too much to ask him if she could sleep in his bed tonight? Would he think it inappropriate? It was difficult for her to say whether or not August was beginning to feel the same way about her as she felt about him, but sometimes, she caught him looking at her in a way that made her think that possibly he had some sort of feelings for her beyond friendship.

Turning over on her side, Mercy stared out the window. It was a long way across the room to see the trees outside of her room, but she needed to focus on something, or else she was going to fall asleep. And falling asleep was never good.

Soon enough, her eyelids began to grow heavy, and she found herself drifting off into a dream. Like so many of the other dreams she'd had recently, she found herself in a dark, damp place, huddled up with her knees to her chest, her arms wrapped around her legs, and her face buried in her knees.

Above her was what appeared to be a lid. She knew this without even looking up. It was always there. Whenever she gathered the courage to lift her head and look above her, she knew she would see nothing but black, nothing but darkness.

It would have been easier to sit there with her eyes closed and her head down. Marcy knew the only way she was ever going to get out of this hole was to face the monster on the other side of that lid.

Something was different this time. She wasn't sure why she thought that was the case, but as she opened her eyes and looked at her own knees, she realized that there was definitely something different about the predicament this time.

"This is a dream." Mercy thought about the power of her own words and what that meant. If this was a dream, then that meant whatever lie on the other side of that lid could not hurt her. And therefore, if she were to stand and attempt to open the lid, she could find out what was on the other side without fear of being hurt—or dying.

She took a deep breath. It would have been easier to do this if she had someone with her, Someone that she could trust. Someone that cared about her. But in here, all alone in the dark, she had no one. She had to rely on herself. She was the only one who could get herself out of here.

Sucking in as much air as she could manage, Mercy lifted her hands above her head and placed them on the bottom of the lid. It was made of wood. She could feel the splinters against her fingers and the roughness against her palms. Without standing, she could place both hands on the lid and press up. That's just how small the space was.

CHAPTER 38 TRAPPED INSIDE

Mercy

The lid to the box wouldn't budge, no matter how much leverage Mercy used with her legs, pushing up from the floor, trying to get the top to open up. Frustrated, she sank back down to the ground, her arms aching.

There had to be a way to get out of here!

She was dreaming. That cognizant thought came back to her. She was dreaming--and she knew she was dreaming. So wouldn't that mean she should be able to get out of here? Shouldn't she be in control of what happened in her own mind?

Looking up at the lid of the box again, she concentrated on it, willing it to move. "Open!" she whispered. "Open, now!" It didn't move. A little louder, she demanded, "Open! Open right now, damnit!"

The box lid still didn't move. Mercy wrapped her arms back around her legs. Why was it that even in her own dreams she couldn't overcome this horrific environment?

As she sat there, fuming, she felt a tingling in her hands. Other memories came back to her. The television she'd made explode. The soda can she'd erupted all over the living room. If she could do those things, she could make the lid open, couldn't she.

"Open!" she shouted. Lifting her hands, she pointed them at the lid of the box, near the crack where the light appeared and disappeared. "Open!"

Blue light began to glow from her fingertips. It was a soft glow at first, but then, as she acknowledged it, the light intensified. "Open!" Lightning bolts left her fingers, shooting up into the lid. The smell of burning wood caught her lungs, and she could see the area of the box where the blue light was touching began to blacken and turn to ash.

Still, the lid itself wouldn't move.

Hot tears began to roll down Mercy's face as she lowered her hands and dropped her head again. It just didn't make any sense. Why didn't her powers work on this box? Why was she even here to begin with? Who had put her here, and how could she get out?

If she knew she was dreaming, then she should be able to manipulate the dream and find a way out. Yet, she was just as powerless in the dream as she was in real life.

If she couldn't get out of the box, maybe she could at least wake herself up from the dream.

"It's just a dream," she told herself. "You're sleeping. You're in a room in Alpha August's house. You're safe. You're fine. It's just a dream. Open your eyes!"

Her view didn't change. She was still staring at her own knees, the sight blurred by her tears. Every breath still smelled of the damp, cedar smell of the box. She was cold. She was alone.

"Why can't I just wake up?" she shouted, lifting her head to look up at the lid again. "You don't control me! I'm not yours to keep in a box anymore!"

"That's where you're wrong!" Suddenly, she heard a male voice booming from outside of the box. "I will always control you, Mari. You will always be trapped in my box. Even when you're not here anymore, I will keep your mind locked away in this box. You can't escape it--you can't escape me."

The lid of the box slowly started to open. Just a crack of bright light leaked in at first, a sliver at best. But then, as the man continued to lift the lid, more light poured in, stinging her eyes. She raised a hand to shield them. Her tears of loneliness and frustration turned into tears of pain from the brightness.

A man was there, looking down at her. From this vantage point, he looked huge. Cast in shadow with the light to his back, she couldn't make out his features, but she knew he was gazing down at her, which made her feel even smaller. "You'll never escape me," he said, and then a wide smile formed on his mouth, and he turned his head just enough that the light from behind him caught his features.

Mercy knew him. She recognized him! It was that man--the one that used to hurt her so badly!

His hand reached into the box, and Mercy began to scream.

CHAPTER 39: SHE-WOLF

AUGUST STOOD AS STILL AS HE POSSIBLY COULD. HE'D TAKEN precautions to hide his scent, but it wasn't always one hundred percent foolproof, so there was a chance the female wouldn't come, or if she did, she might smell him and run. He didn't think she'd see him, though. He was sitting beneath a pine tree that was set on an angle from where he'd seen the female earlier in the week.

Ever since that spotting, he'd had his patrols out looking for signs of her. So far, none of them had seen her, but he thought she might be too afraid to come close with so many wolves nearby. Perhaps she would come if she didn't sense a pack.

Even if he did see her, he wasn't sure what he would do. He would have to be in his human form to talk to her, and he didn't think he could catch her without being a wolf. If he was in his wolf form, he'd have to cross the creek to get to her. That would mean he'd be leaving his pack lands, and that was never safe either.

But he really wanted to speak to her.

She had to know something.

The fact that she was coming so close to his pack made him think that she wanted to communicate with someone about Mercy. Either that, or she was out looking for the other woman. But she had to know that Mercy wouldn't be out here, wouldn't she? Unless she thought that Mercy would want to leave their pack.

If she remembered everything, would she want to leave? He had to hope not, but there were still so many holes in her history, he had no idea what she would think of his pack if her memory was restored. Black Hole Moon had always been a rival pack.

His thoughts were interrupted when he saw movement across the creek. August held his breath, waiting. He didn't want to make any noise at all if he could help it.

He saw her. It was the same wolf he'd seen before. He recognized her dark, matted fur and her eyes. She was standing near the location where he'd spotted her last time, just gazing across the creek into his lands.

'What was she doing?' he wondered. 'Why would she just stand there?'

He had no idea how long she might stay. It was difficult for him to decide whether or not he should approach her, but he knew he couldn't let her get away either.

Slowly, August walked out from behind the trees.

She heard him before she saw him. Her head turned, and then her eyes widened.

She was going to bolt. He knew that expression.

Sure enough, he was only about four steps out from behind the tree when she took off, heading back across Black Hole Moon lands. He needed her to stop. He could probably catch her, but he didn't want to scare her, and he certainly didn't want to hurt her.

So he shifted. "Stop! Please!" he shouted. "I want to talk to you!"

She continued to run, not slowing down.

"Please! Do you know Mari?"

The other wolf stopped and slowly turned back to look at him.

The answer was yes. He could tell by her expression. But she wasn't coming back his way.

"She has amnesia. She doesn't remember much of anything. Only her name. Please. She needs your help."

She was hesitating. He could see it on her face. August prayed she'd come back to him. What else could he say to make her come back? He didn't want to mention Mari's magic in case that was a secret. So all he could say was, "Please. If you care about her, please help us."

The female wolf took a few hesitant steps back toward him. He took a deep breath, thinking that she was coming back to him, that she was going to speak to him.

In the distance, behind the female, August heard a loud, angry howl.

Once again, she turned around and ran away from him, not looking back.

CHAPTER 40: OUT OF THE BOX

Mercy

THE DREAMS WERE BECOMING MORE FREQUENT, MORE INTENSE. EVERY night, Mercy dreamed that she was stuck in that box, and then the shadow man appeared above her, and she screamed louder, and then she woke up. Most nights, it brought August running to her room, rocking her, until she was calm again. She'd usually manage to fall back to sleep, but it was always a fitful, restless sleep.

Isabell had offered her some sleeping medicine. Mercy had been tempted to take it, but ultimately, she'd passed. It wasn't that she didn't think it would help; she was pretty sure it would. She just didn't like the idea of it putting her into such a deep sleep that she couldn't wake herself up, in which case she might end up stuck in the dream that had been tormenting her for weeks.

Then one night, the dream changed. Rather than Mercy waking up the moment she saw the man's face, she screamed, but he reached down, grabbed her hair, and pulled her out of the box by that hunk of hair. The pain radiated all through her scalp.

He tossed her down on the ground and kicked her in the side. Her ribs hurt, and it knocked the breath from her lungs.

"What are you screaming about, bitch?" he shouted. "You stupid whore! What's the matter? Your magic can't save you now, huh?"

Mercy wanted to use the power within her to make him explode, the same way she'd blown up the television and the soda can, but for some reason, she couldn't get her magic to work here, and she didn't know why.

The man grabbed her by the back of her head and tugged her up the stairs. She clawed at his hand, trying to get free, but she couldn't. It wasn't until she was upstairs in what appeared to be a kitchen that he threw her back down on the ground--hard. Her face hit the floor, and her teeth went through her bottom lip, puncturing it. The taste of blood filled her mouth.

"Now, bitch, you're going to do what I told you to do, got it? I'm going to take you over to that asshole's house, and you're going to do it this time, and if you don't... I'm going to knock your teeth down your throat and throw you back in the box for another month, got it? Don't you dare try to hurt me or get away from me either or else you'll pay with your life, and you know it. All I have to do is push this button in my pocket, and you're dead, bitch. You're dead."

The tears were streaming down Mercy's face as he picked her up and moved her to the door. She didn't want to go, but she didn't want to stay.

She didn't want to hurt anyone, but she didn't want to hurt anymore either.

He pushed the door open, and the sun blinded her. She glared against the bright light, unable to lift her hand to shield her eyes because of the way he was gripping her hair.

Her bare feet hurt on the rocks. She wanted to run away from here, to never see this horrible man again.

If only her father knew what he'd done....

He led her to a house across the village and pulled her head back so that she was looking right up at the sky. "All right, bitch. It's time." He lowered his face so that it was right next to hers. "Do it. Do it!"

Mercy took a deep breath as he reached for her wrists. It was then that she looked down to see the chains--the silver chains--around her wrists, and she realized why her magic wouldn't work.

He unhooked one arm and then the other.

Mercy looked up at him, raised her hand and--

She woke up, gasping for air, sitting in her bed in Augustus's house, her heart hammering in her chest. Tears were still streaming down her cheeks, but she wasn't screaming.

At least this time she wasn't screaming.

CHAPTER 41: SOBS

AUGUST

WAKING TO THE SOUND OF MERCY SCREAMING WAS SOMETHING August was growing used to, unfortunately. But hearing her cry was something else completely. When he'd first opened his eyes, he'd been confused about what he was hearing. It was so muffled, it was really difficult to hear at all, and he sort of wondered how something so quiet had woken him up. But then, he was so in tune with her sleep cycles at this point, he might've woken up even if she hadn't.

Running into her room while she was screaming was one thing, but Mercy wasn't screaming this time, so he wasn't sure whether or not he should walk in or just leave her be. After ten minutes of hearing her cry and realizing it wasn't getting any better, August got up. He took the time to put his slippers on this time, something he didn't normally have time to do, and then he walked down the hall.

Her door was closed, so he knocked on it. Since she was awake this time, there was no reason to barge in.

"Y-yeah?" Mercy said between sobs.

"It's August. Can I come in?"

"Uh-huh," she said, her breath staggering and vibrating in her throat.

He pushed the door open and saw her sitting there looking so sad and vulnerable. "Hi."

Mercy swiped at her eyes with the back of her hand, but those tears were quickly replaced by others. August came in and pushed the door closed behind him. "Sorry I woke you up," she said.

"Nah, it's okay. What can I do?" He couldn't help but go to her. He was so used to wrapping her up in his arms and holding her until she was calm, he felt that he needed to do it now, even though she wasn't so out of control that he thought she might literally blow something up like she was most nights.

She didn't answer verbally; she just reached for him, and August sat on the side of her bed and wrapped his arms around her. Her body felt so small against his chest, and he wished that he could protect her with his physical strength all the time, but he couldn't. All of her demons were in her mind.

Running his hands through her hair in an attempt to soothe her, August felt her heart hammering against his chest. "Was it a different dream this time?" he asked quietly, not sure if it would do her better or worse to talk about it.

"Yes. It was so real, too. It's already starting to fade. I just remember wanting my dad. And there was this man. The one I never see. He pulled me out of that box and took me outside, telling me I had to do something. And... my magic wouldn't work. I can't remember why."

"It was just a dream," August reminded her. "He said the same thing every night."

"It was a dream, but it wasn't just a dream." Mercy lifted her head and looked at his face. "It was also a memory. I just have pieces, August. I don't have it all."

He lifted his hand to her cheek and wiped a tear away with her thumb. Even though she'd been crying, she was so beautiful. Her eyes twinkled in the dim light, and her full lips quivered slightly, forming a pout. "I know, Mercy. But you will. One day, it'll all come back, and then you can put it all behind you and move on. You'll never have to worry about any of that again."

"What if…." She stopped talking and lowered her head so that he could no longer see her eyes.

"What if what, Mercy?" August slipped his hand beneath her chin and gently lifted her face so that she was looking at him again.

She took a deep breath and sighed, her entire body shaking with the release. "What if… when I remember who I was before, it turns out… I wasn't a good person? What if I did bad things? What if Rider's right and he's telling you the truth?"

August started shaking his head before she even finished speaking. "No, Mercy. That's not possible. You're not a bad person. I know that."

"How do you know?" she asked, challenging him. She stared into his eyes and asked again. "How do you know, August?"

"I know because…." He stopped. The words weren't coming out of his mouth. He knew he wasn't going to be able to answer that question with mere words.

August leaned toward her, stopping just short of meeting her lips with his. He couldn't just kiss her without her permission, but how could he blurt out the question? He couldn't, so he waited.

Mercy's long eyelashes brushed his face as she held her breath. He moved a fraction of an inch closer to her, and Mercy lifted her face, moving toward him. His lips brushed hers, and then there was no reason for words. She just knew.

CHAPTER 42: TAKE ME

Mercy

AUGUST TASTED EVEN BETTER THAN MERCY HAD IMAGINED HE WOULD. All of these weeks of being so close to him and longing for his touch, to feel his hands on her skin, to taste his lips, and finally, here he was, kissing her, his strong hands on her body as she leaned into the kiss.

In the back of her mind, a voice insisted that this was wrong, that she shouldn't be doing this with a man she just met, especially when she truly didn't know if there was someone else. What if she had a husband back in her old pack? What if she was in love with someone else?

But with August's tongue tapping against hers and his hand on her waist, the other on the side of her face, Mercy knew she wasn't going to be able to stop herself.

Her response to him was completely instinctual, like he was a raging fire and she was a moth, mesmerized by the dancing flicker before her. How could she tell her body not to lean into his? She may as well tell her heart to stop beating or her ears to stop hearing. She had no control over any of it.

At first, his kisses were soft and slow. They were measured. As if he was afraid she might shatter into a thousand shards of glass with just the smallest amount of pressure. But as she ran her hand through his hair and tugged him closer to her, he understood that she wanted him just as badly as he clearly wanted her.

His chest was solid marble. Sliding her hand down his pecs to his abs made her heart race. August slid his hand up to her ribcage, and Mercy found herself whimpering slightly, longing for more. When his hand moved higher to comply, and his thumb found her nipple through her nightgown, she gasped. She couldn't imagine that she had ever felt this good in her entire life.

He wasted no time lifting her nightgown from her and then lowering his head to take her breast between his lips. Mercy tangled her hand in his hair, pressing him further against her. She wrapped a leg around his hips, pulling him closer so that she could reach for the waistband of his pants. He pulled away from her only long enough to discard them, and then he was on top of her, only the thin silky fabric of her panties between them.

August lifted up off of her for a moment to pull her panties out of the way, but before he lowered himself back down on top of her completely, he looked into her eyes again. Mercy nodded and wrapped her arms around him, pulling him to her.

He entered her with a twist of his hips and a timid thrust. Mercy closed her eyes and tipped her head back, feeling herself stretch to accept him. Flashes of this happening with someone else came to mind, but she couldn't see his face, and something told her it didn't feel this good. Not physically; not emotionally. No, the feelings she had with August were wonderful and perfect in every way. She couldn't imagine anyone else ever making her feel this way.

The two of them moved together as one, her lifting her hips as he thrust into her. Mercy felt wave after wave of euphoria wash over her as her mind started to slip away. All she could think about was how amazing her body felt, how incredible August felt inside of her, and how safe she was beneath the shelter of his body.

She felt her muscles begin to tighten and then go into spasm around him as she slid over the edge into ecstasy. Mercy dug her fingernails into his back, panting and calling his name as he kept her there for so long, she had no idea how much longer she could take it. The pleasure was so overwhelming, she wanted to beg him to stop but she also never wanted him to let her go.

Eventually, she felt August tighten up on top of her and knew he was almost at his peak as well. Right as she expected him to fill her with his warmth, he pulled out of her, spilling his seed on her abdomen and in his hand instead of inside of her. At first, she was confused, but then she realized they hadn't used protection at all, and this must be a way he was hoping to prevent her from becoming pregnant. He didn't know that she couldn't have kids.

She couldn't have kids. Why did she know that? Was she sure?

Mercy's eyes were wide as she tried to remember how she knew that and why it was that she couldn't.

"Mercy? Are you all right? Did I hurt you?" August's eyes were narrowed as he leaned down over her, brushing her hair back.

"No, no, I'm fine," she assured him, shoving that troublesome out of her mind as she concentrated on how amazing her body felt and how incredible this man truly was.

"Are you sure?" August asked her. She could tell by his expression that he was already beating himself up for what had just happened as if he had taken advantage of her, and that certainly wasn't the case.

"I'm sure," she told him. She reached over and grabbed some tissue to clean up the mess and then wrapped her arms around him, hoping he knew that she wanted him to stay.

August lay down next to her and pulled her against his chest. Mercy settled against his shoulder, so glad he was with her. "Don't leave, okay?" she whispered to him.

"I won't leave," August promised her. "I'll never leave."

CHAPTER 43: THE NEXT MORNING

IN THE KITCHEN, SIPPING A CUP OF COFFEE, THE MORNING LIGHT streaming through the window, August was left to his own devices. Had he done something as diabolical as it seemed, or had he done the right thing in answering the call he'd been hearing ever since the moment he met Mercy?

He hadn't left until after Mercy had woken up and went to take a shower, but then, she hadn't come downstairs, so he wondered if she'd ended up going back to bed or if she was waiting up there for him to leave.

Maybe she didn't want to see him.

He certainly hadn't gone into her room with the intention of making love to her, but once they'd begun kissing, it seemed evident that the feelings they had for one another were mutual. He'd known the moment that he'd met her that she was special, and not just because of her powers or her beauty. She was made for him in a way he'd never known anyone to fit with another soul. It was as if they were locking pieces of the same puzzle.

Still, she had been out of her element for so long, he felt as if he'd done something wrong by responding to the physical call his body had felt from hers.

The sound of footsteps brought his head around, but he knew that it was his mother before he even looked in her direction. "Good morning, honey," Isabella said, going about fixing her own coffee. "How did you sleep?"

"Fine, Mom. How about you?" He wasn't about to offer up to his mother the fact that he'd slept with Mercy.

It didn't matter. She could tell without him even opening his mouth anyway. Isabella stood next to the counter while her water heated, watching him. She was never one for using the fancy coffee maker. "How is she?"

He shrugged. "She's okay, I think. I'm not sure."

His mother nodded and didn't say anything else until after she had fixed herself a cup of coffee and an English muffin. She brought it over to the table and sat down. "Honey, I'm sure that whatever happened, it's not something you should be feeling guilty about."

"You're probably right, Mom. It's just… she's so vulnerable."

"You didn't take advantage of her. I raised you better than that." She took a bite of her muffin and chewed it slowly.

August knew he hadn't taken advantage of Mercy in the obvious sense of the word, but that didn't mean that he hadn't influenced her to do something she otherwise wouldn't. "I just don't know where her head is at right now, Mom. And what about her past? How do I know she isn't married? What if she has kids?"

Isabella shrugged. "You don't know, I guess. That's the hazard of caring about someone with amnesia. At any moment she could remember that she's already in love with someone else. But… she seems to care an awful lot about you, and she needs someone to love her now, August. I think you've had feelings for her since the moment they found her."

He nodded. His mother knew him well. "I have."

"So… why would you deny those feelings?"

"Because I need to do the responsible thing and put my own feelings aside."

Isabella leaned over and ran her hand through her son's hair before patting him lovingly on the back. "I love you, honey. You're a good kid–a good man. Whatever happens between you and Mercy, I know that you will do right by her. If she has someone else, then, I am sure you'll help her reconcile what she needs to do, and if she doesn't, and the two of you end up together, then I think that will be wonderful for both of you."

August smiled at his mom, so glad to have her words of positivity, even if they didn't quite ease the tension he felt within himself. "Thanks, Mom," he said. He needed to head to the office to see how the evening patrols, but first, he was going to go upstairs and speak to Mercy–no matter how uncomfortable that might be.

CHAPTER 44: AWKWARD

Mercy

Mercy had stood in the shower for a really long time, not sure why she wanted to keep the water running over her body. It wasn't as if she felt dirty, but she did feel guilty. She wasn't sure why she felt that way either. They were two adults. They had been with one another consensually. So why in the world did she feel bad?

Mercy got out, dried off, and got dressed. She still had the towel wrapped around her body when her reflection in the mirror caught her attention. Her hair was starting to grow out more and more each day, and she could see her roots. The odd black color was also starting to fade away. She tipped her head forward and pulled on her hair a bit, trying to look more at her real hair. Why had someone tried to hide it? Had that someone been her?

She also looked at her body. She was so scrawny. Granted, since she'd gotten here, she'd started to put on a little weight. She wasn't quite so bony, but she could still see her ribs, and her arms looked a bit too much like chicken wings. Why would August even want to see her naked?

She made a face at herself and got dressed, knowing she was just being ridiculous. What was truly bothering her was that she didn't even know if she had done something wrong. She didn't know if she had hurt someone else through her actions because she had no way of knowing if she had another man in her life.

Once she was dressed, Mercy walked out of the bathroom and sat down on the end of the bed. She could still smell him. Not in a bad way, but August had a distinct manly smell that always lingered when he was around, and she could smell it now. It was a mix between the woods and ocean, and she loved it. She wanted to fall back into it and wrap it around her.

A soft knock at the door sent her heart racing, and she realized part of the reason she could smell him so well was probably because he was standing outside of her door. "Yeah?" she said, wondering what in the world he wanted. Did he come back to tell her he was sorry, and he knew he'd made a huge mistake?

The door opened, and August stuck his head inside. "Hi. Do you have a minute?"

"Sure," she said, not sure if she should smile or keep a straight face. She couldn't read his expression. He looked friendly but not particularly giddy.

August came in and sat down next to her at the foot of the bed. He cleared his throat and offered her a small smile. "How are you?" he asked.

"Fine," Mercy said with a nod. "How are you?"

"Good. Good," he said, also nodding. "Are you... okay?"

Assuming he was asking if she was physically okay, she said, "Yeah. I'm fine."

"Cool. That's good. Well, I just wanted to make sure that everything was all right because of... uh... I mean... I've got to go to the office. And if you weren't okay, I wanted to make sure that I knew that. So I could help you. To be okay."

It seemed like he was feeling just as awkward as she was. At least, his words implied that he was feeling that way. "I'm fine," she reiterated.

"Perfect." August took a deep breath in and slowly let it out. "Well, if you decide that you're not okay or something, let me know. All right?"

"Yep," Mercy said. This had to be the world's most awkward conversation.

"All right." He sat there a moment longer before he finally got up and started to walk to the door, slowly.

As he walked by her, Mercy wanted to reach out and take hold of his arm. She wanted to pull him to her, to remind him that he said he'd never leave. She wanted to stand up and let him pull her to his chest, to crush herself against him, to declare her love for him and beg him to say the same.

"I'll see you later," August said.

"See you later."

CHAPTER 45: THE STORY

HE NEEDED TO FIND THE OTHER FEMALE WOLF.

Now, more than ever, it was important that he speak to her about Mercy. He needed to know if she could tell him anything about her past. What if Mercy had a husband or children or someone waiting back in that pack for her?

If that was the case, he'd just complicated the situation far beyond measure.

August waited in his human form for her. It had been several days since he bothered waiting out here for her, and now that he and Mercy had been together, he felt more compelled than ever to do what he could to help her figure out her past.

Hours passed by–hours that he could've been using serving the needs of his pack. In a way, he knew he was being very selfish. He was still reachable by the mind-link, and from time to time, his pack mates or his Beta would ask him a question, but mostly he was a man in a field doing nothing but waiting, and he felt like a bum doing nothing.

But he also knew what he was doing was important. If he had to sit there for the rest of the day, so be it.

His waiting finally paid off just before the sun started to set when he saw the female wolf come out of the woods. She looked around and then stepped behind a tree, and for a moment August panicked, thinking she might be about to flee again, but then she came back, in her human form, dressed in a long gown, and August quickly came out of his spot too.

She hurried to her side of the river, and August did the same. "We don't have much time. Listen, Mari came to our pack about three months ago. She was purchased by our Alpha to punish people he didn't like. He kept her locked in a cedar box in the basement and only taken out when he needed her to hurt someone. But one day he must not have gotten the box closed tightly, and she managed to get out and run away."

August nodded. "Why did he dye her hair?"

"Her power is in her hair. When it's the right color, she has the most power. When it's black, it's not as powerful."

August couldn't imagine what Mercy's strength might be like when her hair wasn't dyed then. "Where did she come from?"

"A pack to the north. Silent Moon. Her father was the Alpha. He sold her to Alpha Rider because Mari refused to marry Alpha Peter of their ally pack, Great Moon."

August's eyes widened slightly. He knew Alpha Peter. He had to be at least sixty years old. "He sold his own daughter?"

The woman nodded. "I've got to go, but that's really all I know anyway. Alpha Rider doesn't talk about it much. I know he wants her back, though. He's planning to come and take her from you. He spent quite a bit of money on her. He knows you have her."

"How do you know all of this?"

"I'm his housekeeper," the woman replied.

"Listen, if you want safe passage, I'll give it to you."

He could tell by her eyes that she was considering it, but she shook her head. "I have a family."

"Get them. All of them. I can keep you safe. My army is stronger than his, and he knows it. That's probably why he hasn't attacked yet."

"You're probably right there. He's likely coming up with something else, something you won't be expecting."

August nodded. "Then I guess I'll have to be ready for anything."

CHAPTER 46: TELLING MERCY

Mercy

SOMETHING WAS DIFFERENT.

The moment that August walked into the house, Mercy could tell that something had changed. The weight in his eyes was unsettling, and when he looked at her, she felt like she needed to sit down.

She felt like she needed to melt into the floorboards.

"What is it?" she asked. "Did something happen? Is something wrong?"

"Nothing is wrong," his mouth told her, but his eyes still said differently. "But we need to talk."

"Did… something happen?" she asked.

August shook his head and came to her where she stood at the kitchen counter. She'd been cooking. Not that it was something she was good at, but she'd been trying. She had to wonder if she'd ever even done it before, but she knew how to read, so she could follow a recipe, or at least she thought she could.

"Can you go to the living room, or is there something in the oven?" he asked her.

Mercy's eyes went to the counter. Half of the ingredients for a cake were in a bowl. The oven was preheating. She turned it off "No, I can leave the room," she said, abandoning the project for now.

He led her into the living room and sat her down on the couch so that their knees were touching. Even with the heaviness in his expression boring down on her, she still found some solace in the comfort of his touch.

"Listen, Mercy, I want to tell you some information that I found out today, but I don't want you to get upset, all right. I want you to know that whether or not you remember anything, you're safe here. I want you here, with me. I care so much about you, all right?"

Mercy nodded, feeling fear course through her veins. "You found out about me?"

"I found out some things. I'm just afraid… whatever I say is going to trigger other thoughts and they might be painful or scary."

"And you think I might make something explode?"

"It's possible. I'm not worried about things, but I am worried about you. Whenever that happens, you end up bleeding, and I don't want that to happen, so just try to breathe and be careful, all right, sweetheart?"

Again, she nodded and took his hand. "Do you know where I came from?"

He nodded. "Yes. Your home pack is called Silent Moon. Does that sound familiar?"

"Silent Moon?" Mercy thought it over, saying the name again and again in her mind. "No, I don't think so."

"It doesn't?" He was surprised.

"I mean… maybe, but I don't know. That's my pack?"

He nodded. "I met a female pack from Alpha Rider's village, and she said he bought you from Silent Moon. You were sold to Alpha Rider because you refused to marry Alpha Peter from Great Moon pack. None of that sounds familiar?"

Mercy said those words over and over in her head. Silent Moon. Should that mean something to her? It didn't. Great Moon? Alpha Peter? She closed her eyes, trying to conjure up an image to go along with those words, but they may as well be any combination of letters and sounds. She shook her head. "It means nothing to me."

"Okay." August seemed perplexed. "Well, she also said that he kept you in a cedar box in the basement and that he dyed your hair because that somehow nullifies your powers. Listen, Mercy. I don't know if you're still blocking all of this or if she's just a liar, but I plan to contact Silent Moon and see if what she said is true. Is that all right with you?"

"Why?" Mercy asked, her eyes widening as she looked at him.

"Why... what?" August asked her, his grip on her hand strengthening.

"Why bother? Who cares? I mean... I don't think it matters anymore."

"It doesn't?"

She shook her head. "No, I don't care anymore, August." For the first time since she lost her memory, she realized she didn't care anymore what it was she was forgetting. "I don't care about my past anymore. I only care about my future."

He still looked confused, but August nodded and said, "Okay then. Whatever you want, Mercy. If you don't want me to call, I won't call."

"I don't want you to call." Somehow, she thought nothing good could come of it.

CHAPTER 47: MORE GUESTS

August sat in his office, staring at his phone, wondering if he should keep his promise to Mercy and not make the calls he had planned on making or go ahead and call her home pack and Great Moon as he had planned. He understood that she said she didn't care about her past anymore, but he had to wonder if she would ever be truly safe here as long as those other packs were out there wondering what had become of her.

Once they found out that she was there, with him, would they come for her? Should he arrange to make some sort of trade for her? Clearly, she was valuable. Her powers must've meant something to them. But then, he didn't want Mercy to think that he was trying to buy her.

He didn't think that Silent Moon would come to her. They had been compensated for her already by Alpha Rider. It was already clear that Alpha Rider intended to come for her eventually. He had to know that she was there, that she was just across the river. The only reason he hadn't come yet was because he was waiting. What for,

August didn't know, but he had all but quadrupled his forces patrolling the borders, especially at night, just to make sure that no one was able to sneak in.

He knew that Mercy's greatest protector would be herself, though. August wasn't about to put her in a cedar box to try and contain her powers, and he wasn't going to dye her hair either. Once it grew out, it would be the color it was when she was born. If that gave her greater power, so be it. Whatever she wanted, that's what it would be.

A quick knock on the door interrupted his thoughts. "Yeah?" he shouted.

Beta Beaux came in. "Sir, there's a woman here–and her family. Three kids. She says that you gave her safe passage. They came from across the river."

Knowing it had to be the woman who'd given him the information about Mercy, August rushed out of his office. "Where is she?"

"In the healing center. They aren't harmed, but your mother wanted to check them over."

August rushed in to find the four of them huddled together on one bed. It was her, all right, and what looked to be her three kids. There was a boy who looked to be about eleven or twelve. His jaw was set in defiance. Perhaps he hadn't wanted to come. A girl of about eight sat holding her mother's hand, and a younger boy was on her lap.

"You came," he said with a smile.

"I had little choice. Someone said they saw me," she replied, her face falling. "I was afraid Alpha Rider might hurt us."

"Where's your husband?"

She shook her head. "He's passed."

"I'm sorry." August wished he hadn't asked. "We'll get you a place to stay. Anything you need."

"Thanks. I appreciate it," she said with a nod.

"Of course."

His mother was checking them all over. "Everyone looks healthy," Isabella said with a smile. She tussled the little boy's hair.

"What's your name?" August asked her.

"Aletha," she said. "This is John Junior, but we call him JJ," she said of the eldest boy. "This is Ayla, and the baby is Mark."

August nodded. 'Welcome to our pack. It's nice to have you here. We hope you'll like it here. I'm Alpha August."

At the mention of the word Alpha, fear entered the eyes of the children and they all three reacted similarly to the way Mercy had, dropping down onto their knees. "No," Aletha told them. "It's not like that here, kids. I told you. Alpha August isn't like Alpha Rider. You just need to do this." She made the sign of respect and tapped her fist to her shoulder.

All three kids looked puzzled, but they made the same motion.

August smiled an encouraging smile. "That's right. That's all there is to it. Welcome." The fact that even the children were afraid of Alpha Rider made him want to kill him even more.

CHAPTER 48: PREMONITION

Mercy

Lying in bed next to August was comforting in a way Mercy couldn't quite put into words, despite the fact that she was unsettled deep within her soul. She knew that she would be until something happened between herself and Alpha Rider. August felt responsible for her like it was his battle to fight for her. But Mercy didn't feel that way. She knew she'd have to face him herself, and when she did, she'd have to put the matter to rest once and for all.

August's arm was around her waist, and he had her pulled tight against his chest. Even facing away from him, his manly scent was strong, and she was reminded of the ocean, despite the fact that she had no idea if she'd ever actually been there or not. Coming to grips with the fact that she didn't have to remember what had happened to her before or where she'd come from had given her a sort of freedom she hadn't expected before, but at moments like this, she wished she knew if the images of the ocean and the beach that filled her mind were from her past or just from television shows and photographs.

Mercy closed her eyes and tried to go to sleep, but she kept thinking back to what August had told her before he went to sleep, that Aletha and her children, a family from Alpha Rider's pack, had shown up that day. Mercy hadn't gone to see her yet, even though Aletha said she knew who Mercy was. She was the one who'd told August all of the information he knew about her past. Mercy thought it best to give Aletha a few days to get assimilated. Then, she would go and see her. It wasn't as if Mercy would remember her anyway.

At least, she didn't expect to recognize her. She didn't expect to have any memories of the woman whatsoever. If she did, that would be a good thing, she supposed. But… that probably wouldn't happen.

Eventually, Mercy dozed off, but her dreams weren't peaceful. No, they were anything but. Instead, she saw herself walking on a battlefield. All around her, there were fallen wolves. She was in her human form, though. Her hair was long and blond, the way it should be. She was wearing a flowing red gown, and she could feel her powers flowing through her. Occasionally, an electric flicker would flow through her hands so that she could see it in the air.

In the distance, she saw Alpha Rider, also in his human form, walking toward her. How she knew it was him when she didn't remember what he looked like, she couldn't say, but it was him. It was time. She was about to show him what happened when someone attempted to mess with her powers. There was no hair dye, no cedar box, nothing to dull her power. He had nothing to protect him from her.

And yet, he was confidently walking toward her, an arrogant grin on his face, as if he knew something she didn't know. The smoke from the battlefield curled around them, and Mercy found herself looking in around, searching for something, someone.

August. Where was he? Did she even know what he looked like in his wolf form? Wouldn't she know him anywhere, in any form?

Alpha Rider had almost closed the distance between them, and whatever it was that had him so amused, she was about to call his bluff. Mercy raised her hands, blue light pulsing between her fingers, ready to end this once and for all….

Catching her breath, Mercy sat up in bed, the dream over. Her heart was pounding in her chest, but she realized it was just a bad dream. Her eyes went to August. He was asleep. He was fine. She closed her eyes for a second, thankful that it was just a dream.

But she knew, just like those other dreams were memories, this one wasn't just a dream either.

It was a premonition.

CHAPTER 49: COFFEE WITH A STRANGER

Mercy

ALETHA DIDN'T LOOK FAMILIAR TO MERCY AT ALL. IN A WAY, SHE WAS A little relieved when she walked into the cafe to find the woman and didn't recognize her. Aletha waved her over to her table, greeting her with a smile, and Mercy said hello back, shaking the hand that was offered to her, but the face she was staring at may as well have belonged to someone she'd never met before in her life. Just like every other face she'd seen since she arrived here.

"So... where are your kids?" Mercy asked as they both sipped the drinks the waiter brought to them.

"Alpha August got them settled in school this morning," Aletha explained. "It's different here than it was in the old pack. I don't have to teach them myself." Aletha smiled and took a sip of her coffee.

Mercy smiled and nodded as if she knew the difference, but she didn't. She didn't have kids herself, so she hadn't really done much to investigate how school worked here, and she had no idea how it had worked at their old pack. "Do they like it here?"

"So far," Aletha said. "They love the new cabin. We have television, which is amazing. They could watch it all day if I let them. And the options for food are all different. When I told Ayla she was allowed to wear pants if she wanted to, she almost died."

Mercy raised her eyebrows in concern until she realized Aletha didn't mean it literally. She meant her daughter was happy that she didn't have to wear dresses. "That's good. I'm glad they like it here. I like it, too."

"It's hard to believe that two packs could be so different from one another when they're located so close to one another. I know that your pack was very different, the one your father is Alpha of, but it was so far away."

"I don't remember," Mercy reminded her. "And if I'm honest, Aletha, I don't want to remember. I told Alpha August I don't want him to do any investigating into my past anymore. I'm just happy to be here."

Aletha stared at her for a minute. "But you do know... Alpha Rider's not going to be content with letting you stay here, right? He'll come for you." She had her voice low like it was a secret. Mercy could see not wanting to alarm the other patrons.

"I'm not too worried about it," Mercy told her, though that wasn't completely true. The dreams she'd been having recently, about facing Alpha Rider on the battlefield, didn't end with her winning. Not that she ever saw the end. But she got the impression that he had a card up his sleeve that was going to keep things from turning out the way she hoped.

Her eyes still wide, Aletha said, "I'm not sure that's the best attitude to have, Mari. I mean, Mercy. I know that your powers are strong. But Alpha Rider has his way of finding the things he needs in order to get his way. If he wants to find a way to get you back, he'll figure it out."

Mercy kept the smile on her face. "We'll see," she said. "So... do you think you'll work while you're here?" She figured changing the subject was the best way to handle the current topic of conversation.

Aletha was having a hard time letting the topic go. Her eyes lingered on Mercy's for a moment before she blinked several times and then said, "Uh, yeah. I'm going to start working in the cafeteria at the school. Alpha August helped me get the job. He thought it would be perfect because then I could check in on the kids during the day. I start on Monday."

"That is great," Mercy said, taking another sip of her coffee.

"What about you?" Aletha asked her. "Will you start working at some point?"

Mercy shrugged. "I've offered. They won't let me."

"Oh." Aletha looked like she had something else she wanted to ask, and Mercy thought she knew what that question was–was there something going on between her and Alpha August. But since Mercy wasn't quite sure what the answer was, she didn't want to encourage Aletha to ask the question.

All she knew was how she felt about him. When she was with him, she felt like she was flying. She wanted to wrap her arms around him and never let him go....

"Mercy, are you all right?" Aletha asked with a bit of a crooked grin on her face.

"Yeah, I'm fine," Mercy said. "I'm just fine."

CHAPTER 50: BATTLE PREP

August

Waiting for an attack wasn't fun. August would've much rather launched one himself. But he had no reason to do so. Not yet anyway. Not according to pack rules. While August could argue that Rider had committed atrocities against pack members, all August had as proof was the word of a couple of ex-pack members. And one of them had amnesia.

On the other hand, not only did Alpha Rider have cause to attack his pack, he was likely to do it at any time. August had already started taking precautions and preparing. He had his Omegas preparing, practicing over time. He also had increased patrols and set up some other lines of defense around the perimeter of the village.

August walked around outside and saw that the trainers were taking a group of Omegas through their paces, getting them ready to fight, not just in case Rider attacked but just because it was something all Omegas needed to be able to do. In fact, in August's pack, even Gammas had to learn how to fight just in case. From the ages of twelve until a shifter turned twenty-one, they had to attend training classes at least twice a week. After that, it was up to them, unless they were an Omega. Then, they continued their training as part of their Omega duties.

"They look pretty good, don't they?" Beaux said, coming up to him. Beaux had also been observing. Why, August couldn't say, but he was glad to have his Beta there to discuss what he was seeing.

"They do," August said, nodding. He took note of one particularly feisty, smaller Omega woman. She couldn't have been more than five feet tall in her human form, but when her sparring partner came near her, she fought the much taller male off every single time. "They're working really hard."

"I know. Paul and Sandy say they've seen a real uptick in the quality of trainees all of a sudden," Beaux said. "Neither of them knows why, but they're pleased with it."

"That is interesting," August said. He had to wonder if it hadn't made it through the rumor mills that there was now a second pack member from the pack across the river in their midst. That might make them more aware of the fact that they could be attacked at any time. "How are the extra patrols going?"

"They're going well?" August asked.

"So far, no one has seen anything on any of their patrols. But then, I have a feeling that when Alpha Rider attacks, he will be practically invisible until he's right on top of us."

August nodded. He had a feeling that Beaux was right, even though he was confident that his Omegas were capable of detecting Rider's men as soon as there was a threat.

In front of him, that feisty female shouted as she spun around and kicked at her opponent, barely missing his chest as he leaped backward out of the way. She brought her other leg around, and almost got him again. They weren't supposed to actually make contact, but she seemed determined to get as close as possible. Her eyes were narrowed, and her teeth were bared.

"She's good," August said. "I hope they can all fight Rider's wolves with that sort of spirit."

"That's Kesha," Beaux said quietly. "She has a habit of accidentally hurting her opponents, so the trainers keep giving her bigger males. So far... Justin's been lucky."

Just then, Kesha brought her boot around and caught Justin in the chest, knocking him backward about ten feet onto his bottom. He was okay, but he was rattled.

Beaux and August exchanged glances. "He might need to ask for another partner," August said, and Beaux laughed.

"Don't worry, Alpha August. When Rider comes, we'll be ready." Beaux looked confident.

"I know you will be," August said. They'd better be because he wasn't letting anything happen to Mercy.

CHAPTER 51: NOT THE LUNA YET

Mercy

WALKING THROUGH THE PACK, MERCY BEGAN TO REALIZE THAT PEOPLE were recognizing her. She wasn't sure how she felt about that. At first, it was odd having people she didn't know greet her by name. But when weeks turned to months, and she began to learn who a few of the people in the village were as well, it became nice to know some of the villagers.

"Good morning, Mercy," Bill, the man who ran the post office said one morning as Mercy went to town to grab some coffee. She found that walking to the coffee shop each morning gave her something to do. Since August still didn't want her to work, she had to find something to keep herself busy. By now, her hair had grown out, and it was almost all blonde. She'd cut the black off as it got longer, and now it was a little past her shoulders, and only the last few inches were black.

"Good morning, Bill," she called back. "It's a nice spring day. I bet that will be nice for your delivery routes."

"It will be," he said. "As long as it doesn't rain this afternoon."

Mercy looked up at the sky and only saw white puffy clouds. "I don't think it looks like rain."

"You never can tell in the springtime around here," he said with a laugh, hurrying on to the post office. She waved goodbye and headed on down the street to the coffee house.

Several more people waved or said hello to her. She thought that it might have something to do with the fact that she lived with the Alpha. Everyone knew by now that she had a special place in his heart. She wasn't sure exactly what was going on between them, but they shared a bed. And she loved him, so there was that. August had never said that he loved her, but she liked to think that maybe he did.

He was still so worried that Alpha Rider was going to show up and try to take her back. Mercy had all but forgotten about that. It seemed like so long ago that she was worried about being taken away from him by that evil man. Now, the only time she ever thought about Alpha Rider was when she had the occasional dream about him.

Those were few and far between, though.

No, she wasn't worried about Alpha Rider. Not anymore. He wasn't coming for her. He probably didn't think about her any more than she thought about him.

Mercy walked into the coffee house and ordered her usual, smiling at the barista, Jenny, whom she sort of counted as a friend. One of these days, she wanted to go out to lunch with a friend. Or go shopping. Or do something else that friends did together like she saw on television shows.

"Here you go, Luna," Jenny said, handing Mercy her drink. "Oh, I'm sorry. I'm not sure why I called you that just yet."

Mercy took her drink. "Luna?" Mercy repeated.

"Yeah. Well, that's what you'll be if you marry Alpha August." Jenny shrugged like it was a given that Mercy and August would get married. "Then, you'll be the one responsible for helping all of the needy in the pack. You'll be so good at that, too."

Mercy wasn't sure what to say. She didn't think she'd be so good at that, but she appreciated the sentiment. "Thank you, Jenny." She smiled and took her drink, turning to go.

It was then that Mercy realized not once had she ever paid for her drink.

CHAPTER 52: HEAVY THOUGHTS

August

SOMETHING SEEMED TO BE BOTHERING MERCY. AUGUST WASN'T SURE what it was, but all evening, ever since he'd come home from work, and they'd sat down to dinner, he'd noticed there was something weighing on her mind.

Recently, his mother had taken to working the evening shifts at the healing center. At first, August had told Isabella that wasn't necessary, but now that he had evenings to himself to share with Mercy, he was sort of glad to have the house to themselves. It was almost as if they were a married couple. Sometimes August almost forgot that they weren't married–that he hadn't even told her how much she truly meant to him yet.

As they finished up their pork chops, which his staff had so excellently prepared for them, he began to wonder if perhaps that was part of the problem. She'd been in his home for so many months now, sharing his bed for a couple of those. Was she beginning to wonder exactly what the nature of their relationship was, or was August reading too much into her expression?

"Is everything okay, Mercy?" he finally asked her as they went into the living room. Most evenings, she would read a book while he watched whichever sporting event happened to be on television.

"Yeah, everything's fine," she said with a tight-lipped smile that told him everything was not fine.

August raised an eyebrow and tried to determine whether or not he should push the topic. After all, if she wanted to tell him what was truly bothering her, she could have, right?

But as she sat in her usual chair with a blanket draped across her lap, her book open but none of the pages being turned, he had a feeling that she was tempted to talk to him about whatever it was that was bothering her.

"Are you sure you don't want to talk about it, Mercy?" August asked, turning the volume down on the TV. "Whatever it is, even if I can't help, I don't mind listening."

She smiled at him and flipped her blonde hair over her shoulder. She looked so different now than she had when he'd first met her, with that cropped black hair. But she was beautiful no matter what her hair looked like. "Well, it's just... do you know Jenny at the coffee shop?"

"Sure," August said with a nod. He knew pretty much everyone in his pack. "What about her?"

Mercy stared at him for a long moment. He could see she wasn't sure if she should tell him. Finally, she said, "Well, I'm sure it's nothing. I probably shouldn't even tell you. It's just... she accidentally called me something today that's been weighing on my mind a lot."

"What's that?" he asked, leaning forward toward her. He hoped Jenny hadn't said anything rude. He couldn't imagine she would. Jenny was a nice person.

"She called me... Luna." Mercy looked up at him through her long eyelashes, and August felt his own eyes widen.

"Oh," he said, looking away. "Oh."

"Yeah. I know. I shouldn't have said anything. It just made me wonder... what everyone else thinks. That's all."

"Right," August said with a nod. "I don't blame you." He managed to whip his eyes back around to face her. He'd never been good at talking about his feelings. He was better at expressing them by showing people how he felt. When he made love to Mercy, he hoped she could tell how he felt about her. But... maybe he needed to tell her.

"So, that's all," she said, shrugging and turning back to her book. She seemed to be putting a period on it, but he knew better. She wanted to know what he thought about it.

Only he didn't know what to think about it. He did think his pack members had a right to know whether or not he intended to ask Mercy to become his Luna–their Luna.

He just hadn't been able to convince himself to put a lot of thought into that because he was honestly afraid of it.

What if she didn't want to be his Luna?

What if she didn't feel the same way about him as he felt about her?

How did he feel about her?

He did know the answer to that question, whether he had put it into words to her or not.

He loved her.

He loved her more than he'd ever loved anyone.

And he wanted her to be his Luna.

So... how did he tell her that?

August had no idea.

But he was going to have to figure it out.

CHAPTER 53: A NEW JOB

Mercy

MERCY PROBLEM SHOULDN'T HAVE SAID ANYTHING. FOR THE NEXT FEW days, August was acting strange, and she knew he was probably trying to figure out how to get her out of his house. After all, she had all but insinuated that she thought she was supposed to be his Luna just because she'd been staying with him.

And sharing his bed.

She felt really silly, though. For all she knew, August slept with all sorts of women in the pack, and she was just the newest of the women he'd invited into his home–and into his bed.

One afternoon, a few days after the conversation she'd had with him, she was in the kitchen, cleaning up, when Isabella came in. "Oh, hi there, Mercy," she said. "August just called. He said that he has something he'd like to talk to you about. Would you mind meeting him at the restaurant downtown?"

Mercy stared at her for a moment. It seemed so strange that August's mother would be giving her such a message. "The restaurant?" she said. "Okay." The cook had already asked if they'd like to have chicken for dinner, and she'd said that sounded fine.

"Yes, that's right. He said to meet him there in an hour. I laid out a dress for you that I think will look nice," Isabella said. She had a little twinkle in her eyes that Mercy couldn't quite understand.

"All right," Mercy said, still confused. She dried her hands and went upstairs, thinking the staff would probably be happy to have her out of the way so they could clean the kitchen properly.

Once upstairs, she went about taking a shower and fixing herself up. She had no idea what August had in mind, but she had to wonder if maybe he hadn't found a place for her to live. Maybe he'd chosen the restaurant downtown because he had asked them to hire her to work there. He'd hardly spoken to her in the last few days since she'd mentioned the conversation she'd had with Jenny at the coffee house, so it made sense that he'd been making arrangements for Mercy, to get her out of his home.

The dress Isabella had laid out was lovely. Mercy hadn't seen it before. She got dressed, putting on a necklace and earrings and the red heels Isabella had also laid out for her. It wouldn't do not to look her best if August was trying to get her a job.

Could she even work at a restaurant? Surely she could figure it out. She was certain it was more difficult than it looked, waiting tables, but if other people could do it, surely she could, too.

Once she was certain she looked her best, she checked the time. She'd have to walk pretty fast to make it there on time.

As she was walking out the door, Isabella shouted, "Bye, honey. Have a nice time."

"Thank you," Mercy said back and then headed on her way.

When she arrived, she was surprised to see that the restaurant was all but empty. Only the woman who took her to her table and a few other staff members were there. Even August wasn't there yet.

It only took a second for him to walk in, though. Mercy was still getting situated in her seat when the Alpha came in, wearing a suit with a dark-colored jacket and a red tie. He looked so handsome, she forgot all about her guess that he'd been arranging to get her a job.

"Hi, Mercy," August said, his voice as soft as the candlelight flickering for their table.

"Hi," she said, her forehead furrowing as she tried to sort out what was going on. "Is everything okay?"

He didn't answer her. Instead, he cleared his throat and said, "I think I should just go ahead and ask you what I brought you here to ask you before I don't have the nerve to do it anymore."

Mercy continued to stare at him, wondering what in the world he was talking about.

August reached into his jacket pocket and pulled out a small black box as he dropped onto one knee, reaching for her hand. "Mercy, I know we haven't known each other that long, but I've known you long enough to know that I love you, and I have since the moment I met you. I don't need to know your past to understand that I need you in my future. No matter what happens next, I want you to be with me. Will you be my wife–and my Luna?"

Mercy stared at August for the longest moment, unable to believe that he was actually asking her the question that was coming from between his lips.

She still didn't remember her past, but none of that mattered now. Only he mattered. Only her future mattered–their future.

"Yes," she said. "Of course, I'll marry you. I love you, too."

August slipped the ring on her finger, and Mercy leaned down as he came up to meet her, his lips enveloping hers.

He had brought her there to find her a job, and she'd gladly accept the job of pack Luna, even if she had no idea how to do it. If it meant being August's wife, she'd figure it out.

CHAPTER 54: SEALED WITH A KISS AND MORE

Mercy

That night, once dinner was over, August took Mercy back home to their room and the bed they'd been sharing for months. It all seemed different now, though, now that he had asked her to become his wife, to be his Luna. His kisses were somehow even sweeter, and every touch of his hands on her flesh was even warmer, alighting her flesh on fire.

August stood behind her, his arms wrapped around her, his lips playing with the sensitive flesh between her neck and shoulder as he slowly tugged down the zipper on the back of her dress. Mercy had kicked her shoes off already, and when the top of the dress came loose, she worked her arms out of the short sleeves. August's lips worked their way down her neck and across her shoulder. She leaned back against his muscular chest, her eyes closed so she could concentrate on every touch of his hands on her skin.

The dress came off and puddled on the floor at her feet. He slid his hands inside of her bra, causing her peaks to harden instantly at his touch. She let out a soft moan, and her hands raised to cover his, holding him in place as he continued to lightly pull and pinch, driving her mad.

When he pulled his hands away to unhook her bra, she hated to let him go, but it only took him a moment to take the garment off and toss it aside. Mercy turned to face him, and his lips devoured hers. August lifted her, dropping her backward onto the bed as Mercy's fingers fumbled with the buttons of his shirt. He had his shoes off, and she was able to get his shirt off quickly enough. She ran her hands along the surface of his chest, sliding them down across his hardened abs, finding his belt and quickly unbuckling it.

August lowered his head and took a nipple between his lips. Mercy bit down on her bottom lip as waves of pleasure washed over her. She unhooked his pants quickly, and he worked them off, taking his boxers with them so the only scrap of garments either of them had left were her thin, wet panties.

He hovered over her for a moment, looking down at her and smiling. Mercy lifted a hand and ran it through his hair, caressing his cheek. Sometimes, she still couldn't believe how lucky she'd been to have been found by him—to have found him.

Lowering his face to hers, August kissed her again as he hooked his thumbs through her panties and tugged them off. Mercy lifted her hips to assist, and then, when he plunged deep inside of her, she lifted to meet him, relishing in the feel of him as he filled her completely.

"I love you so much, Mercy," he whispered against her ear as he worked his hips, thrusting in and out of her.

"I love you, too," she managed to whisper, despite the fact that her breath was caught in her throat and her mind was slipping away. Every muscle in her body was responding to the pleasure August sent rippling through her.

"I'm so glad you're going to be my wife, going to be my Luna," he continued.

All she could get out in response was an ethereal moan as August ground against her most sensitive spot, taking her to the edge of euphoria and sending her toppling right over.

He held her there for quite some time before he joined her, too, and then she felt his warmth radiate throughout her. "I love you," he said again.

Mercy opened her eyes to see August looking right at her. He saw her like no one ever had before. Even if he hadn't known who she was before, it didn't matter. He knew who she was now. And he loved her.

She loved him, too, more than anything.

CHAPTER 55: BEING THE LUNA

Mercy

The view out of Mercy's window was beautiful. August had given her an office that looked out on a meadow, and sometimes, she would stare out the window and daydream about how beautiful their wedding had been and how lovely it had been to take a week off and just spend time with her new husband.

Mercy hadn't wanted an elaborate wedding, but everyone in the pack was invited since August was the Alpha, and Mercy was becoming the pack Luna. Still, they were able to keep the ceremony itself relatively short. After that, they'd gone straight into a ceremony to name her as the Luna. The reception had been long, but the happy couple had not stayed for the entire time. They'd danced a bit, ate some food, thanked all of their guests, and then gotten straight to their honeymoon.

Now a few weeks later, here Mercy sat, staring out at a beautiful spring day, wondering how she got to be so lucky.

Being the Luna was exactly how Mercy thought it would be. It was challenging, but it was so very rewarding. Helping people was something she found that she was good at. Just as so many pack members had come to her aid when she'd needed it most, once she became pack Luna, she was able to help so many people.

Her favorite part of her job was helping children. When a parent came in and asked her to help their children either with a medical need that the pack could fund or with some sort of material need the family couldn't afford, Mercy was always keen to help them with whatever funds she had allocated to her.

Isabella had trained her for a few days, but after that, her mother-in-law had walked away saying, "This woman was born to be a Luna. She doesn't need my help."

Occasionally, Mercy's mind would wander to what her life might have been like before she came here to be with August, but it never stayed on her mind much at all. It was inconsequential now. Whatever her past was, it was over. Now, she was here, with her new husband and her new pack. She was making friends and proving herself to be an asset to her pack. That's all that mattered.

She never used her powers anymore. She never needed to. It had been months since anyone had startled her and she'd accidentally used them. Just like her past, her abilities became something she rarely thought about.

"Are you daydreaming again?" August asked in a teasing voice as he came up behind her and rested his large hands on her shoulders.

Mercy laughed and placed her hands on top of his. "Possibly," she admitted. "I'm sorry. I just can't help but think about how lucky I am to be your wife." She tipped her head up, and he leaned down and kissed her. "Why are you home early?" she asked, checking the clock. It wasn't the time that he usually came home.

August shrugged and came around to lean against her desk. "Nothing much was happening in the office, so I came home to be with you."

Mercy's smile widened. She loved being home with August. As much as she'd liked the little trip they'd taken for their honeymoon to a cabin in the mountains, just staying at home with him was vacation enough. Now that Isabella had moved out, they had some privacy, and they often ended up kissing–or more–whatever room they were in.

"Do you have work you need to finish?" August asked her.

Mercy looked down at her desk. "Nope," she said. "Nothing that can't wait."

"Good," he said, taking her hand and pulling her out of her seat. "Then... let's go do something fun."

"Did you have something in mind?" Mercy asked, giggling as she walked along with him.

August smiled at her, and she knew exactly what he had in mind without her husband saying a word.

Regardless of what her life had been like before, it was pretty perfect now.

She hardly ever thought of Alpha Rider anymore.

Hardly ever.

She did wonder, though, if he ever thought of her.

Something told her that he probably did....

CHAPTER 56: KNOCKS IN THE NIGHT

Mercy

She was dreaming about Rider again.

Mercy was walking through the battlefield, the smoke blowing around her, bodies lying randomly around her feet. Her eyes were fixed at a distant point where she knew he would appear.

Only this time, unlike all of the other dreams she'd had, Alpha Rider wasn't showing up, and she didn't understand why.

As she continued to search for him, her mind wandering, trying to sort out where he might be, where Alpha August might be, she began to hear a banging noise to her right. It was a rhythmic noise, but the longer she walked, the more persistent she became until she finally realized it wasn't part of her dream.

"I'm dreaming," she reminded herself.

Mercy sat straight up in bed. August was up, too, and he was pulling on some clothes over his boxers. Someone was banging on the door downstairs, hard. "Who is it?" she asked him.

"I'm not sure, but something's going on," he said. "Stay here."

"Why would I do that?" she asked, getting up and rushing to the closet to get dressed as August headed downstairs.

Mercy grabbed a pair of joggers and yanked them on beneath her nightgown. She grabbed a sports bra out of her top drawer and stripped off her nightgown, pulling on her sports bra and then pulled on a T-shirt over the top before she hastily shoved her feet into some sneakers and rushed down the stairs behind August, working her hands through her hair as she went.

There was a warrior at the door, a man named Steven. "They took us by surprise," he was explaining to the Alpha. Should we sound the alarm?"

If Steven was asking the Alpha to sound the alarm, then it was bad. "Yes, sound the alarm so the children can take cover," August told him. "Call all warriors to the point of contact immediately. Get the rest of the guards on patrol. I want to make sure there's no other infiltration."

"Yes, sir," Steven said with a nod. Then, he rushed off into the night.

August turned around and looked at Mercy. He sighed and his face softened. "I thought I told you to stay in bed."

"And I thought I said no," she said with a shrug. "What's going on? Who are we being attacked by?"

He didn't answer for a second, and in that second, she knew who it was. "Alpha Rider," he said quietly.

"So… after all of this time, all of these months, he's finally come for me?" she asked him.

"Not necessarily," her husband said. "He's hated us for years. There's a chance this has nothing to do with you."

Mercy scoffed. He didn't know, though, about the dreams. She hadn't told him about all of the times she'd dreamed all of those nights about Rider facing off against her on the battlefield. "He's here for me, August."

"Well, then," he said, stepping over and running his thumb across her cheek. "That means we need to hide you away somewhere where he can never, ever find you."

"No," Mercy said, shaking her head. "I can't do that. I won't let other people fight my fights for me, put themselves at risk while I lock myself up, August. I'm going out there with you."

"Mercy—"

"Stop," she said, putting a finger to his lips. "I can take care of myself."

He reached up and gently removed her hand. "You haven't used your powers since you got here. What if you don't remember how to use them?" he asked.

He had a point, and judging by her dreams, there was a good chance she didn't know how to do it.

"I'll figure it out."

August was shaking his head no, but he didn't have any choice. She was going. One way or another.

CHAPTER 57: NIGHT BATTLE

August

It was no wonder that Rider had been quiet for so long.

He'd been training his warriors.

He'd been collecting more.

As August made his way across the battlefield, it was clear that his enemy had been working hard to prepare himself for this night. Everywhere the Alpha looked, he saw his Omegas fighting with Rider's ferocious wolves. Blood, sweat, tufts of fur, claws, and fangs…. It was a vicious battle, one of the worst he'd ever seen, and August was afraid to see the aftermath.

If he survived the night.

Before August could even think about what he needed to do next, a large male wolf stepped before him, and he found himself engaged again. It wasn't the first time he'd had to fight instead of simply directing his warriors that night. He'd already dispatched four other wolves, and if he wanted to get back to overseeing the battle, he'd have to do the same to this large black wolf as well.

Saliva hung from the wolf's teeth as he stared at August, his eyes glaring with menace. August wasn't about to wait for the other wolf to make a move. He might've been slightly larger, but that didn't mean he was going to easily defeat August.

The Alpha got down low and charged at the bulky wolf, sweeping at his legs and taking his front left out from underneath him. The other wolf growled and tipped to the right, snapping at August with his teeth, but he didn't care. He easily dodged away from his bite, flipping his head around and managing to sink his teeth into the wolf's shoulder. He yelped in pain but pulled away.

August let him go but not for long. Using his back legs, he launched himself up into the air and pounced, scratching at the other wolf whose claws came around and slid into August's right shoulder. It stung, but it didn't stop him.

Slipping out of his grasp, August dodged around behind him and managed to use his leverage to tip the wolf backward. Now, he was off-kilter, and there wasn't much the larger beast was going to be able to do to regain the upper hand, not without help, and a quick glance around told him that no one was coming.

Acting quickly, August let his instinct take over. He aimed for the other wolf's neck, sinking his teeth down into the throbbing vein he could sense pulsing right beneath the surface there, the fur and flesh not masking it from him. Tearing through the muscle, his teeth bit through, and the warm, salty blood of his enemy rushed into his mouth. It was never a pleasant taste, but August got over it when it meant surviving to live another day.

He pulled his mouth away, taking a big chunk of the other wolf's neck away with him. He spit it out quickly and then went in again to finish the wolf off quickly. There was no sense in watching him suffer. With another bite to the jugular, the wolf began to bleed out quickly, and as August stood over him, struggling to catch his breath, the dark wolf stilled.

The Alpha took a look around. He needed to find Rider. If he could kill the other Alpha, he might be able to put an end to this madness.

At least he knew that Mercy was home, tucked away, safe, and she hadn't come out in this. She'd wanted to, but he'd talked her out of it. This was his war to fight. He would keep her safe, no matter what. And when this was over, she wouldn't have to worry anymore. Not about Rider. Not about anyone.

CHAPTER 58: NO MERCY

Mercy

AUGUST HAD MADE HER PROMISE TO STAY IN THE HOUSE, AND MERCY had pretended to comply. It was better that way. Well, it was easier that way, anyhow.

When she stepped outside, about an hour after the battle had begun, she knew exactly what to expect.

She wasn't wearing a long, flowing gown like she had been in her dreams, though. She was wearing a much more practical outfit. She had on pants and they were tucked into her boots. She was also wearing a long-sleeved shirt. It was a bit chilly in the predawn hours. A light fog hung over the village. It was fog–not smoke.

Why would it be smoke? It wasn't as if wolves fought with weapons that fired gunpowder like humans did. Still, she did smell smoke in the distance. As she began to walk toward the sound of fighting, the smell became stronger, more acrid, and she realized that there were some buildings on fire on the perimeter of the village.

That bastard Rider had set some of the villagers' homes on fire.

Mercy shook her head and knew that this needed to be stopped now.

Not a lot of memories lingered in her mind, but she did have plenty of physical responses to pull from that told her what she needed to do. The best way to deal with Rider was to deal with everyone all at once.

Mercy reached the edge of the battlefield and stopped. She saw wolves engaged in battle all around her. It was difficult to tell who was winning, but it didn't matter. She knew that she could end it all without anyone else having to get hurt on either side, and she had a feeling that the wolves fighting for Rider's side didn't want to be there either.

Mercy looked around to make sure she wasn't in any immediate danger, and then she closed her eyes. Using her power, she felt out around her and sent out a pulse, one that she hadn't used in months, maybe years. She felt the energy leave her body in a massive wave. The ground shook beneath her feet, and a hush fell around her. The sounds of snarls and growls in the distance stopped. When she opened her eyes again, no one was moving—no one.

She hated to do that to the warriors on her own side, but she knew she hadn't done any long-term damage to them. With any luck, they'd recover quickly and get up, hopefully before the others.

Now, she needed to find Rider.

She knew he would hang back, stay out of her range. He would be aware of what she could do, of what she would do, so he wouldn't be close enough for it to affect him. No, the other Alpha wouldn't be lying on the ground, waiting for her to sneak over and jam a knife in his throat. No, he'd be waiting.

Waiting for her.

As Mercy headed out to find him, she absently wondered where August was. She imagined her husband was somewhere lying on the ground unconscious with everyone else. If Rider were able to hurt or kill her, if he could capture her, August would be next. Rider would find him and kill him before he even opened his eyes. Then, he'd kill everyone else in her village.

Mercy wouldn't let that happen. When she found Rider, she'd make sure he understood, in no uncertain terms, that this was over.

When she'd first arrived in the pack, she'd been given a name that reminded every one of her kindness, but it wouldn't reflect her actions that night.

No, this time, she would show no mercy.

CHAPTER 59: FACE OFF

Mercy

It didn't take long for Rider to come into view. He was about a quarter of a mile ahead of her, in between some trees, just stepping out of a clearing.

Of course, he would be hiding from the battle, Mercy thought.

He stepped out into the field. The fog curled around him, just as it had in her dreams. He was in his human form, just as she was, and for once, Mercy wished she hadn't forced herself to wake up before the dreams had ended.

At least then maybe she'd have some idea what was about to happen.

Rider wasn't alone.

It took Mercy a few seconds to realize that there was another person following him, but when her eyes locked on the blonde woman behind him, a rush of memories came back to her, and she suddenly realized she knew exactly who she was.

She looked so much like Mercy, even from a distance, she could tell that they resembled one another. It was almost like she was looking in a mirror. Except she was shorter and a couple of years younger.

She was wearing a flowing gown, the same one that Mercy had been wearing in her dreams.

Was it possible that it wasn't her that was walking among the fallen at the end of the dream–but her sister?

"You came!" Alpha Rider came, his arms spread wide. "For a while, I was beginning to think perhaps you wouldn't."

"This is over, Rider," Mercy said, keeping at least twenty yards between them. "Why is she here?"

"Why not?" he said. "You didn't want to do your job, but she does."

Looking at her sister, Leeta, she said, "You don't have to do this. You're free to go." Her hair was long and blonde, which meant her powers would be free-flowing.

But she had never been as strong as Mercy, not unless Rider had found a way to make her more powerful.

"I don't want to," she said. "Rider is my husband now. We are happy together. I've come to make you pay for running away from him and for disappointing Father."

Once again, Mercy was bombarded with memories. This time, it was her cruel father's face that filled her mind. She remembered how he'd sold her to an older Alpha, and when she'd refused to go, she'd ended up with Alpha Rider.

"Leeta is prepared to do whatever it takes to bring you in with us, even if it means destroying your new pack," Rider said.

"She's not as strong as I am," Mercy told him.

"I don't know about that," Rider said, his smile crooked. "She's been practicing."

Leeta formed a ball of blue energy in her hands and made it float there for a moment.

Mercy didn't let it bother her. "So have I," she said. "Leeta, I don't want to hurt you. You're my sister."

Scoffing, Leeta flicked the ball of energy at Mercy. It came flying at her, turning into a bolt of power as it neared her. Mercy was able to use her own powers to move it aside, but it was clear this was going to be quite the battle.

"Fine," Mercy said. "If you want to fight, I'll fight. But you remember, you asked for this."

Leeta smiled, and another ball of energy came flying at Mercy.

This time, she stepped aside and formed her own energy ball. But she didn't send it at her sister. She knew that it was Rider that she'd have to bring down if she wanted to end this fight. She threw it at Rider.

Leeta put up some sort of shield that kept her powers from affecting the Alpha, but it definitely took a lot out of her sister to try to do both, shield her husband and create a blast at the same time, and she wasn't going to be able to do both simultaneously for long.

Mercy didn't let down. While Leeta was still trying to recover from deflecting that last blow, she sent another wave of energy headed in their direction. Leeta again defended against it and sent a blast at Mercy. This one singed her hair as it went over her head, but Mercy wasn't bothered by it. She ducked out of the way of the fireball and sent more pulses of energy their way, knowing that that was more powerful than a simple fireball.

Her sister was beginning to crack. Not only did Leeta know it, so did Rider. He took a few steps back toward the tree line, like he was about to run off and hide. "Come on, Leeta!" he shouted, hitting her in the shoulder. "What's wrong with her?"

"I'm trying!" his wife told him.

Mercy shook her head. "You're a fool, Rider. You never should've thought she was strong enough to take me. No one is!"

"But… your father said…."

He didn't get to finish his sentence. It was obvious Leeta was about to collapse from sheer exhaustion. Seeing that his plan was failing, Rider did what all cowards do when they're about to die.

He turned around and ran.

CHAPTER 60: TRACK DOWN

Mercy

MERCY HAD A CHOICE TO MAKE. SHE COULD EITHER CHASE RIDER DOWN and destroy him, or she could stay there with her sister who had collapsed on the ground but could get up at any moment and begin to wreak havoc on the sleeping wolves that Mercy had immobilized earlier.

She couldn't leave the wolves unprotected, but she also couldn't let Rider get away.

With no other choice, Mercy hit her sister with a jarring bolt of energy, one that was sure to keep her from getting up for quite some time. She hated to hurt her own flesh and blood, especially since she was quite certain that her sister was misdirected in the decision she had made, but she had little choice because she couldn't take the risk of Leeta getting up and hurting someone.

Then, Mercy took off after Rider.

She wasn't going to catch him by running after him, though. He was a male, for one thing, so he was naturally faster than her. Also, he was an Alpha, so he was stronger, more muscular, bigger than she could ever hope to be. No, if she was going to get him, she'd have to use the one advantage she had over him—over everyone.

Her magic.

Once she entered the forest, Mercy felt out into the woods for Rider and almost instantly found him about fifty feet in front of her. Using her powers, she sent a pulse of power toward him. She heard him shout as it hit him, and then she began to reel him back in.

As she pulled him to her, she continued to walk forward until she saw him. He was still struggling, trying to get away from her, but there was simply no way he was going to be able to get away from her power. She was far too strong for even someone of his girth to break free from her.

Mercy wasn't even breathing hard. She wasn't getting close to maximizing her powers. She could've handled more if more was thrust upon her.

Once Rider was back to her, she dropped him onto the forest floor and stepped around so that she was in front of him so that if Leeta was able to get up and started coming that direction, she'd see her.

"Please, Mari," he said, "just let me go back to my pack, and I'll never bother you again. I promise."

"It's too late for that," Mercy told him. "You should not have come here. You should've left well enough alone."

"I realize that now," he said. "Please… just let me go."

She shook her head. "No, I won't let you go. But I won't be the one to decide what to do with you either."

"What are you talking about?" he asked.

Without answering him, Mercy picked him up off of the ground using her magic and walked him back to where she'd left the wolves.

When she exited the woods, she expected to see her sister still lying on the ground.

But Leeta was gone.

Rider began to laugh. "She's gone. She probably has August by the balls right now."

"Not after seeing you turn tail and run," Mercy said, but she was worried. She knew her sister was almost as foolish as Rider. It was possible she was doing something stupid at the moment.

Picking up her pace, she hurried back to the battlefield, looking for August.

It wasn't hard to find him. He was still in his wolf form when she spotted him, and he was only slightly conscious.

And Leeta had a knife to his throat.

CHAPTER 61: BATTLE'S END

Mercy

"Put him down, Leeta," Mercy demanded. "Unless you want your husband to explode all over the place. Put that wolf down."

"That wolf?" Leeta repeated. "Isn't this your husband? The Alpha?"

"No," Mercy lied, hoping she'd buy it. "You've got the wrong one. That's just an Omega." August didn't even look like a random Omega, but her sister wasn't the brightest, perhaps she'd fall for it.

"Don't listen to her, honey," Rider shouted. "That's Alpha August.

"Says the man who left you and ran away only a few minutes ago. I could've just killed him in the forest, but I didn't," Mercy reminded her sister.

"Why didn't you?" Leeta asked. "Why didn't you just kill him while you could?"

"Because they call me Mercy now," she explained. "I want to live up to my new name. I wanted to give my husband the opportunity to spare yours."

Leeta pressed the knife so that a drop of blood appeared on August's neck.

"Don't!" Mercy yelled. "If you kill him, you know I'll kill Rider."

"Then let him go, and I'll let August go. Then we can both go on about our ways," Leeta proposed.

"But how will I know that you won't come back here, looking for me again?" Mercy could see that August was beginning to come around now, and if she kept her sister talking, it wouldn't be long until her husband could overpower her sister.

"We won't," Leeta told her. "We promise."

"Oh, well, as long as you promise," Mercy said, sarcastically.

"Can you distract her?" August asked in her head.

"Yes," Mercy told him. To her sister, she said, "Don't you remember what Dad used to say, Leeta?"

Leeta looked confused. "Do you remember? I thought you had amnesia.

"Oh, come on, Leeta," Mercy said, "surely, you remember."

Leeta shook her head. "I don't know what you're talking about.

Rider was clearly getting tired of hanging there. "Just end him already, Leeta," he said.

"You know, Rider, I think you should stand over here," Mercy said, moving him to the other side of her, drawing Leeta's eyes away from August.

"No!" her sister shouted as she followed her husband with her eyes. It was exactly what August needed. He was much more awake than he was pretending to be. Just as he lunged to bite the hand that was holding the knife, Mercy sent another disabling pulse at Leeta so that she couldn't move, and his teeth sank down into her hand.

Leeta screamed in pain. August didn't bite down too hard, but let go as soon as the knife was loose. The other wolves on the battlefield were beginning to awaken now. August was more awake than the others, thanks to the jarring sensation of being held at knife point, but as Rider's wolves saw the situation, they stood, eyes wide, wondering what to do.

"Surrender!" Mercy shouted. "Surrender, or I kill him!"

One by one, the wolves dropped to their knees, surrendering to Mercy and her overwhelming power so that Rider wouldn't be killed and the rest of them wouldn't be hurt either. It was quite clear the woman with the magical powers wasn't messing around.

As August's Omega warriors came back around, they began to shift and get dressed so that they could deal with the Omegas from the attacking pack. Mercy wasn't sure if they'd all be taken prisoner or if they'd be released, but it didn't matter to her. The battle had ended, and they were victorious.

It was over. It was all finally over. Rider was in custody, and Mercy knew he'd never be able to come and hurt her again.

August was still in his wolf form, but he looked at her from across the battlefield, and Mercy smiled at him, feeling relief wash over both of them.

EPILOGUE

Mercy

"MERCY, HURRY UP!" AUGUST SHOUTED UP THE STAIRS. "WE'RE GOING to be late!"

"We can't be late," Mercy shouted back to him. "They can't start without us. You're the Alpha."

"Well, we're supposed to be there in fifteen minutes, and it'll take at least ten to get to the chapel."

"I'm coming," Mercy said, sliding an earring into her ear and looking at herself one more time in the mirror. What her husband failed to realize was that she not only had to get herself ready, she also had to get the baby ready, and that took some time.

She looked good in a nice red dress and silver dangling earrings. She wore a pendant around her neck that had a picture of August in one half and her daughter in the other. Her hair was up in a clip, and her knee length red dress was tight at the top but flowy at the bottom. Her red heels were not so high that she couldn't walk in them easily.

She hurried down the stairs to see August standing at the bottom of the stairs, holding their daughter, Abigail, in his arms. The baby was wearing a red dress the same shade as her mother's. Her hair was styled with a headband with a bright red bow, and she smiled when she saw her mother.

One of her black shoes was on the floor.

"She lost a shoe–again," Mercy said.

"She's always missing a shoe," August said.

Mercy bent down to pick it up and worked it back onto her daughter's foot. "This is why I'm always late."

"At least the diaper bag is ready. Isn't it?" August asked.

"Yes," she assured him. She'd taken care of that earlier in the afternoon.

Once Abigail's shoe was on, they hurried out the door and headed for the chapel. It was a very important day for their family.

Today was Abigail's dedication ceremony. She'd be recognized as the daughter of the Alpha and Luna of the pack and next in line to lead the pack.

The only way she wouldn't be is if they had a son and Abigail decided to let her brother be Alpha.

But Mercy would never ask her daughter to do such a thing.

"You look beautiful," August said, kissing Mercy's cheek.

"Thank you," she told him. Satisfied that they had everything they needed, they headed out the door, rushing to the chapel so as not to be late for their own ceremony.

As they walked, Mercy thought about how far they'd come. She'd been found in a heap of leaves in the forest and brought to August. He'd taken her in and taught her to love herself as well as falling in love with her himself.

They'd fought Rider and his pack and brought them to justice, He was locked up in a dungeon below the jail. Her sister had been returned to her father's pack. She knew better than to ever show her face there again.

Mercy felt confident that they no longer had to worry about anyone attacking them. She was free to enjoy her family. She was free to use her powers and be herself.

As they walked into the chapel, everyone greeted them, including

August's mother, whom they'd taken to calling Grandma Isabel. She gushed over Abigail. The little girl reached for her grandmother, and as she did so, her shoe fell off.

Mercy sighed and went to pick it up, but before she could do so, the shoe floated up off of the floor and went right back onto her daughter's foot.

Shocked, Mercy turned to Abigail, wide-eyed. "Did you do that?" she asked.

Abigail giggled.

"You didn't do that?" August asked.

"No," Mercy replied.

August sighed. "Great. Looks like I get to live with two magical women."

Mercy laughed and the family moved in to take their spots so that Abigail could undergo her dedication ceremony.

Like mother, like daughter, she supposed. At least she knew that she wouldn't have to worry about her daughter protecting herself. Not that her father would ever let anything happen to her.

As she sat in the chapel pew next to August with his arm wrapped around her, Mercy couldn't help but feel completely blessed to be found by the Alpha.

ALSO BY ID JOHNSON

Stand Alone Titles

All I Want for Christmas is Pooch

(*sweet contemporary romance*)

Christmas Memory

(*sweet contemporary romance*)

The Doll Maker's Daughter at Christmas

(*clean romance/historical*)

Pretty Little Monster

(*young adult/suspense*)

The Journey to Normal: Our Family's Life with Autism (*nonfiction*)

Found by the Alpha (*fantasy romance*)

Love Throughout Time

(*time travel romance*)

Back to Titanic

Back to Gettysburg

Back to Bunker Hill

Back to the Highlands

Back to Port Royal (coming soon!)

Silverwood Academy

(*paranormal romance*)

Vampire Hunter

World Builder

Realm Jumper

Celestial Springs

(psychological thriller/literary fiction/women's fiction)

Beneath the Inconstant Moon

The First Mrs. Edwards

Leaving Ginny

The Motherhood

(dystopian romance)

Rain's Rebellion

Rain's Run

Rain's Return

Ashes and Rose Petals

(contemporary romance/retelling of Romeo and Juliet and Cinderella)

Girl in the Attic

Girl From the Tomb

Girl On the Beach

Nashville Country Dreams

(contemporary romance)

Meant to Marry Me

Lead Me Home

You Are the Reason

Forever Love series

(clean romance/historical)

Cordia's Will: A Civil War Story of Love and Loss

Cordia's Hope: A Story of Love on the Frontier

The Clandestine Saga series

(paranormal romance)

Transformation

Resurrection

Repercussion

Absolution

Illumination

Destruction

Annihilation

Obliteration

Termination

A Vampire Hunter's Tale (based on The Clandestine Saga)

(paranormal/alternate history)

Aaron

Jamie

Elliott

Christian

The Chronicles of Cassidy (based on The Clandestine Saga)

(young adult paranormal)

So You Think Your Sister's a Vampire Hunter?

Who Wants to Be a Vampire Hunter?

How Not to Be a Vampire Hunter

My Life As a Teenage Vampire Hunter

Vampire Hunting Isn't for Morons

Vampires Bite and Other Life Lessons

Gone Guardian

Death Does Not Become Her

Blood of the Vampire Hunter (based on The Clandestine Saga)

(paranormal romance)

Night Slayer

Shadow Stalker

Queen Catcher

Mother Hunter

Father Finder

Ghosts of Southampton series

(historical romance)

Prelude

Titanic

Residuum

Lusitania

Heartwarming Holidays Sweet Romance series

(Christian/clean romance)

Melody's Christmas

Christmas Cocoa

Winter Woods

Waiting On Love

Shamrock Hearts

A Blossoming Spring Romance

Firecracker!

Falling in Love

Thankful for You

Melody's Christmas Wedding

The New Year's Date

Charles Town Brides (based on Heartwarming Holidays Sweet Romance)

(Christian/clean romance)

From This Moment

Can't Help Falling in Love

<u>It's Your Love</u>

<u>When You Say Nothing At All</u>

<u>My Girl</u>

<u>Unchained Melody</u>

<u>I Only Have Eyes For You</u>

<u>At Last</u>

<u>The Very Thought of You</u>

Reaper's Hollow

(paranormal/urban fantasy)

<u>Ruin's Lot</u>

<u>Ruin's Promise</u>

<u>Ruin's Legacy</u>

When Kings Collide

(steamy historical romance)

<u>Princess of Silence</u>

<u>Princess of Hearts</u>

Collections

<u>Ghosts of Southampton Books 0-2</u>

<u>Reaper's Hollow Books 1-3</u>

<u>The Clandestine Saga Books 1-3</u>

<u>The Chronicles of Cassidy Books 1-4</u>

<u>Celestial Springs Collection</u>

<u>Heartwarming Holidays Sweet Romance Books 1-3</u>

<u>Heartwarming Holidays Sweet Romance Books 4-7</u>

Websites: https://books2read.com/ap/xX7ZD8/ID-Johnson

For updates, visit www.authoridjohnson.blogspot.com

Follow on Twitter @authoridjohnson

Find me on Facebook at www.facebook.com/IDJohnsonAuthor

Instagram: @authoridjohnson

Follow me on Bookbub: https://www.bookbub.com/authors/id-johnson